A massive fist rocketed toward the Executioner

Bolan whipped the Beretta into target acquisition, but a rock-hard fist slammed into his forearm. The blow jarred the 93-R from his numbed hand.

Levi Birnbaum's face was bruised and bloodied, but his eyes burned with rage. He'd lost his Uzi but climbed the hill to confront the Executioner, armed with only his exceptional strength.

A big fist rocketed toward Bolan's face, but the warrior dodged the punch and lashed out with his foot, striking Birnbaum in a kidney. The terrorist groaned and lunged, hands clawing for his adversary.

Bolan recoiled, then threw an overhead right at the man, his knuckles striking Birnbaum in the cheek. The blow stunned the big terrorist, but didn't hurt him. The warrior followed through with a kick to his opponent's heart.

The Samson leader hissed with pain and swept an arm at the Executioner, which hit him in the chest like a hammer, lifting him off his feet and dumping him on his back.

Sensing victory, the enemy moved in for the kill....

MACK BOLAN.

The Executioner

#130 Dead Line	Stony Man Doctrine
#131 Ice Wolf	Terminal Velocity
#132 The Big Kill	Resurrection Day
#133 Blood Run	Dirty War
#134 White Line War	Flight 741
#135 Devil Force	Dead Easy
#136 Down and Dirty	Sudden Death
#137 Battle Lines	Rogue Force
#138 Kill Trap	Tropic Heat
#139 Cutting Edge	Fire in the Sky
#140 Wild Card	Anvil of Hell
#141 Direct Hit	Flash Point
#142 Fatal Error	Flesh and Blood
#143 Helldust Cruise	Moving Target
#144 Whipsaw	Tightrope
#145 Chicago Payoff	Blowout
#146 Deadly Tactics	Blood Fever
#147 Payback Game	Knockdown
#148 Deep and Swift	Assault
#149 Blood Rules	Backlash
#150 Death Load	Siege
#151 Message to Medellín	Blockade
#152 Combat Stretch	Evil Kingdom
#153 Firebase Florida	Counterblow
#154 Night Hit	Hardline
#155 Hawaiian Heat	Firepower
#156 Phantom Force	Storm Burst
#157 Cayman Strike	Intercept
#158 Firing Line	
#159 Steel and Flame	
#160 Storm Warning	
#161 Eye of the Storm	
#162 Colors of Hell	
#163 Warrior's Edge	
#164 Death Trail	
#165 Fire Sweep	
#166 Assassin's Creed	

DON PENDLETON'S
THE EXECUTIONER®
FEATURING MACK BOLAN®
ASSASSIN'S CREED

A GOLD EAGLE BOOK FROM
WORLDWIDE®

TORONTO • NEW YORK • LONDON
AMSTERDAM • PARIS • SYDNEY • HAMBURG
STOCKHOLM • ATHENS • TOKYO • MILAN
MADRID • WARSAW • BUDAPEST • AUCKLAND

First edition October 1992

ISBN 0-373-61166-8

Special thanks and acknowledgment to
William Fieldhouse for his contribution to this work.

ASSASSIN'S CREED

Printed in U.S.A.

And Samson said, Let me die with the Philistines. And he bowed himself with all his might; and the house fell upon the lords, and upon all the people that were therein. So the dead that he slew at his death were more than they which he slew in his life.

—Judges: 16:30

If lives are taken because of the greed of others, then they become my enemies. And I therefore have no choice but to bring down the house of my enemies.

—Mack Bolan

THE
MACK BOLAN®
LEGEND

Nothing less than a war could have fashioned the destiny of the man called Mack Bolan. Bolan earned the Executioner title in the jungle hell of Vietnam.

But this soldier also wore another name—Sergeant Mercy. He was so tagged because of the compassion he showed to wounded comrades-in-arms and Vietnamese civilians.

Mack Bolan's second tour of duty ended prematurely when he was given emergency leave to return home and bury his family, victims of the Mob. Then he declared a one-man war against the Mafia.

He confronted the Families head-on from coast to coast, and soon a hope of victory began to appear. But Bolan had broken society's every rule. That same society started gunning for this elusive warrior—to no avail.

So Bolan was offered amnesty to work within the system against terrorism. This time, as an employee of Uncle Sam, Bolan became Colonel John Phoenix. With a command center at Stony Man Farm in Virginia, he and his new allies—Able Team and Phoenix Force—waged relentless war on a new adversary: the KGB.

But when his one true love, April Rose, died at the hands of the Soviet terror machine, Bolan severed all ties with Establishment authority.

Now, after a lengthy lone-wolf struggle and much soul-searching, the Executioner has agreed to enter an "arm's-length" alliance with his government once more, reserving the right to pursue personal missions in his Everlasting War.

PROLOGUE

The explosion at the Rishon Hotel, Tel Aviv, occurred without warning. One minute all was tranquil, the next a set of elevator doors on the second floor were torn apart by a blast, cables bombarded by flying shrapnel. One elevator car plunged to the bottom of the shaft when the suspension lines were severed. Screaming passengers felt the ruthless pull of gravity as they suddenly crashed to the basement level. The car protected those within from the full impact of the fall and the metal debris that showered into the shaft.

The occupants of the other elevator were less fortunate. The explosion occurred as the second car was passing the floor to the lobby below. The passengers didn't have a prayer.

Emergency vehicles responded immediately to the explosion. The city was located far from the troubled borders where most of the violence in Israel occurred, yet its defenses remained well honed and primed for emergencies. Police, fire department and state military forces were quick to arrive at the scene. They found dead and wounded, a yawning gap in a build-

ing and charred remnants of destruction—another
scar in a nation that had been marked a thousand
times like a seasoned street fighter.

THE PRESS ARRIVED at the hotel while the emergency
vehicles blocked much of the street. Newspaper reporters parked wherever they could, then rushed to the
scene with microphones and video cameras in hand.
Members of the Israel Broadcasting Authority tried to
claim first rights to the story, but the foreign press
corps wasn't impressed. The journalists from other
lands hadn't come to Israel to admire the Mediterranean. They hungered for a ripe story on the Middle
East. Since the Israeli government had attempted a
media blackout along the troubled West Bank, the reporters had languished in Tel Aviv until the news of a
local act of terrorism.

Reporters fired off questions in half a dozen languages. Policemen and firemen avoided the journalists. A military press liaison officer announced that a
full report of the investigation would be released to
them in the morning. He repeated the declaration in
English as well as Hebrew, but the reporters were dis-
satisfied. They demanded to know if this was an act of
terrorism and the number of victims involved.

"The Palestinians are responsible!" a voice boomed
with anger. "Who else would commit such an atrocity?"

Several reporters recognized the man who emerged
from the crowd of spectators. Levi Birnbaum was a

striking figure. Six foot four and bulging with muscles from daily workouts, he was an impressive slab of brute force capped by a sleek head and fierce features. His dark eyes seemed aglow with rage as he addressed the press corps.

"The PLO struck here tonight because they don't want us to tell the people of Israel the truth," Birnbaum stated in English that barely carried a trace of his Brooklyn childhood. "They're afraid of us because we, the Samson Warriors, have come to urge Israel to take the only course of action that will ensure the Jewish state will not be swept away by an Islamic tide or sold out by its so-called allies."

He stepped closer to the microphones and glared into camera lenses as if defying the glass orbs to disagree. Birnbaum ignored the liaison officer's plea that he hold his tongue. He'd never been one to pass up a TV opportunity, and he had no intention of doing so now.

"This was an act of terrorism," Birnbaum assured the press. "Not just a senseless PLO bombing, but an effort to distract everyone in the hotel while they attacked the real target. Five of my followers are gone. Their rooms reveal signs of struggle and bloodshed. Indeed, they kidnapped my comrades and friends, fellow Samson Warriors who are my brothers as surely as if we shared the same mother's womb.

He thrust a thick finger at the collection of lenses and spoke loudly to be certain every microphone recorded his words. Birnbaum seemed to bubble with fury, and no one present would have been surprised if flames had begun to jet from the man's eyes.

"No doubt the PLO expects me to agree to their demands for the return of my brothers," he announced. "Munir Kmed and his henchmen may hold them hostage or even kill them. I will not back down. My warriors would never forgive me if I did. Our lives aren't as important as what we believe in. We will *not* negotiate with terrorists. We will *not* back down from our enemies. Just as Israel must remain strong and uphold these convictions, it shall be true of myself and the Samson Warriors."

He ended his statement with, "There is only one way to negotiate with terrorists, and that is with a gun in your hand. The only way to deal with our enemies is to destroy them."

1

Hal Brognola stared at the two men in his office, his brows knit in concentration. He chewed on an unlit cigar and drummed his fingers on a stack of file folders.

"Thanks for getting here so fast. I had a meeting with the President and a representative of the State Department a few hours ago," the big Fed began. "Got one hell of a situation in the Middle East."

"That's pretty standard for that part of the world," Mack Bolan stated. "What happened this time?"

"Ever hear of Levi Birnbaum and his so-called Samson Warriors?" Brognola inquired.

"I seem to recall Birnbaum was a member of the Jewish Defense League and left the organization because he didn't consider it militant enough in support of Israel," Yakov Katzenelenbogen answered, taking out a pack of Camels. "He formed the Samson Warriors to endorse stronger military support and foreign aid to Israel. They're regarded as extremists, but I don't recall reading anything that suggests they've resorted to violence."

"Not as a group," Brognola confirmed as he placed his hand on top of the folders. "But these are records of criminal charges and federal investigations of the members of the Samson Warriors. Every one of them has a rap sheet. Birnbaum himself was convicted of assaulting a Saudi diplomat in New York and beating up three Arab Americans who were staging a pro-PLO protest in front of the Israeli embassy in 1989. The FBI still has Birnbaum at the head of the lists for suspects for a bombing incident that killed two Iranian immigrants in Chicago and the unsolved murder of Heinrich Gruber in Pittsburgh.'

"Gruber?" Bolan said with a frown. "The elderly German immigrant who was accused of being a Nazi war criminal? Nobody could supply enough proof that Gruber was guilty, but somebody wasted him in his own backyard instead of waiting for the legal system to deal with the guy."

"Yeah," Brognola stated. "He was nailed with a 12-gauge shotgun. Three bursts of buckshot. Whoever did it wanted to make sure Gruber was very dead indeed. By the way, there's still no evidence the guy was ever a Nazi."

"You've got quite a few files there," Katz remarked. "I didn't think the Samson Warriors consisted of more than two dozen members."

"It doesn't," Brognola replied. "But the guys who belong to it have all served time one way or the other. Most have been convicted for felonies involving violence. One sick bastard spent three years in a state mental hospital for beating up prostitutes and women he *thought* were hookers. Claimed God wanted him to go out and punish harlots. Birnbaum has got himself a real collection of beauties here. They're all nasty and every one of them is probably a fanatic just like Birnbaum.''

"And they're Jewish," Katz commented with a shrug.

"Sorry," the big Fed said. "Guess there are a few wackos in every ethnic group."

"I've noticed."

Katz's career as a commando, espionage agent and antiterrorist had begun when he was a boy, fighting the Nazis in Occupied France. His family had been victims of Hitler's "final solution." After the war, Katz joined the Israeli struggle for an independent Jewish state. He lost his arm in the Six Day War and later became a top operative with Israel's Mossad.

Occasionally Katz was "loaned" to other intel outfits in the United States and Western Europe. Due to his remarkable background, the Stony Man operation had chosen Katz to be the unit commander of an elite antiterrorist squad known as Phoenix Force. After dozens of successful missions, Katz had proved he was still one of the best operatives in the world.

"You mentioned the Middle East, Hal," Bolan reminded Brognola. "What do the Samson Warriors have to do with trouble halfway around the world?"

"Because that's where Birnbaum and his buddies are. The Samson Warriors arrived in Israel two days ago. Apparently they're trying to drum up new recruits there because they couldn't seem to get any more loonies here in the States. Anyway, a bomb went off at the hotel in Tel Aviv where the Warriors were staying. Several people were killed, but nobody's sure who set off the explosion.''

"You think Birnbaum's people did it?'' Katz asked with surprise. "He's a Zionist fanatic. Why would he set off a bomb in the middle of the second largest city in Israel?''

"Beats me. But Birnbaum told the press the bomb was the work of the PLO and that the Palestinians kidnapped five of his Warrior chums right out of their rooms at the hotel.''

"Kidnapped?'' Bolan asked with a frown. "None of these Samson extremists were killed, no bodies found in the hotel rooms?''

"That's right. There was evidence of a struggle in each room, but that could have been done by the Samsons themselves. In short, nobody knows for sure if the men were really abducted or if Birnbaum and his followers are responsible for the bombing and faked the kidnappings. That's why you two are going to Israel.''

"Do tell,'' Bolan said dryly. "This isn't the typical sort of mission we get. Shouldn't the Israeli authorities and the CIA be looking into this?''

"They are,'' the Stony Man chief assured him. "But the President wants us involved, as well. You guys know something about U.S.-Israeli relations. Uncle

Sam gives Israel billions in foreign aid every year. Washington is counting on Israel being our big ally in the Middle East, and Israel would go down the tubes without Uncle Sugar's economic and military assistance.''

"Not everyone is happy with that arrangement," Katz remarked. "A lot of Americans are fed up with seeing U.S. tax dollars—their money—going to support Israel when thousands of Americans are homeless and the U.S. economy is in major trouble that requires an increase of the burden on the taxpayers. Many Israelis aren't happy with what they regard as American efforts to manipulate their country and dictate how Israel should conduct its business."

"Yeah," Brognola said with a nod, "and there's been even more static between the U.S. and Israel lately due to accusations of violations of human rights by the Israeli military against Arabs living in the West Bank. Hell, you guys know what a mess this has been. The President wants us to handle this because we get results, and this is the sort of thing that can best be accomplished by a small team of very good men because they can be both discreet and ruthless if necessary."

"I think I understand," Bolan said with a sigh. "The Samson Warriors are a gang of misfits. Uncle Sam doesn't really want them to come back to America, but Wonderland is afraid they'll be an embarrassment to the U.S. if they start trouble in Israel."

"And the Israeli government might not want them either," Katz added. "But they're still more comfortable with the idea of Palestinian terrorism than acknowledging a group of American Jews as terrorists. Especially a group that supports a stronger military position in Israel and increased U.S. assistance."

"That's about the size of it," Brognola told both men. "There's also the problem that this alleged kidnapping will make the Samson Warriors get sympathy and more support from certain individuals who will immediately believe Birnbaum's claim. Of course, Washington doesn't want to look anti-Semitic by ignoring the Samsons, either. Politicians are sensitive to criticism from ethnic groups...even if the criticism comes from supporters of extremist outfits like Birnbaum's gang."

"There's a possibility Birnbaum's telling the truth," Bolan reminded the big Fed. "There are plenty of Palestinian fanatics in the Middle East, and some of them might have targeted the Samson Warriors. Birnbaum's people are certainly extremists, but that doesn't necessarily mean they're guilty of murdering several innocent people at the hotel just to serve as a front for a bogus abduction claim."

"You see what a mess this is?" Brognola inquired, aware the question was needless. "There are problems with every aspect of this Samson Warriors business. I'm handing you guys a real headache with this assignment. It's your hard luck that you're the best men for the job."

"I've had missions in the Middle East before," Bolan stated. "Nobody I'd rather have with me on this job than Yakov. Unless, of course, you can send all of Phoenix Force with me to Israel."

"The other four members of my unit would be delighted to work with Mack again," Katz assured Brognola.

"And I'd like to give the assignment to them, too. Unfortunately the Israeli government isn't being terribly cooperative, and neither is our own State Department. We aren't getting any official support from anybody. Thanks to Yakov's connections with the Mossad, they're willing to assign a handful of men and some assistance. However, they insist on the smallest team possible from our end. Two men is as small as a team can be."

"Sounds like bureaucrats in Jerusalem are influencing how the Mossad operates," Katz commented with a sigh. "Geller himself might be the problem. I knew him before he became the Mossad director. He was never very trusting of the United States, and he's probably even less so since the U.S. objected to Israeli agents conducting espionage within the United States."

"Stealing top-secret information from the U.S. government and military isn't the sort of thing Uncle smiles happily about," Brognola remarked. "Even if the country that does it is an ally."

"Friends spy on each other and steal from each other," Katz said, shrugging slightly. "That's how the espionage game is played, and it probably always will be. Of course, if one gets caught with a hand in the proverbial cookie jar, one can expect to get one's wrist slapped. Geller isn't the type to look at it that way. He's probably annoyed with the U.S. for even considering meeting with the PLO and for any criticism of Israeli military actions during the *intifadeh.*"

"Why the Israelis want to play the game this way is their business," the Executioner declared. He was a realist and had little interest in politics on any level. "What concerns us is if we can carry out our mission when we get there, or are we going to be bogged down by paper pushers who won't let us out of the airport?"

"You'll have more or less freedom to handle the situation however you see fit," Brognola assured his friend. "Just remember if the heat gets too much for the bureaucrats, they'll ship you out without giving you time to pack your toothbrush."

"What will we be able to pack for the trip?" Bolan asked. "Airport security in Israel is tighter than a miser's purse strings. We won't be able to smuggle weapons and special equipment into the country unless somebody waives customs at both ends."

"The Mossad connections will set you up with everything you need," the Fed promised. "Uzis, most likely. Phoenix Force has been using the mini-version Uzi machine pistol for recent missions. If you prefer the little brother to the standard SMG, Yakov, I'm sure they can accommodate you."

"I'd prefer the full-size model unless we're going to carry a lot of extra gear," Katz answered. "However, I'm accustomed to the Walther P-88 pistol, although I'll use something else if I have to."

"We can send one through the U.S. embassy in Tel Aviv by diplomatic pouch," Brognola suggested. "Striker can get his 93-R the same way. Give me a list, and we'll put all the special items in a single package for the embassy."

"Fair enough," Bolan replied. "Our mission is to find out what really happened in Tel Aviv. If the Samson Warriors were really kidnapped, we rescue them—if they're alive—and return them to Mother Birnbaum, even if they are a pack of zealots. If the Samsons have staged this affair, we nail them and let the Israeli authorities deal with their crimes—providing we don't have to take them out altogether."

"That's right," Brognola confirmed with a nod. "You've got it."

"I know I've got it," the big man replied. "I just hope everybody we'll be working with understands it as well."

2

Mack Bolan grabbed the steering wheel and jerked it to the left. The startled driver gasped and said something sharply in Hebrew. The Executioner didn't understand the man's words any more than the Israeli NCO knew why he had abruptly decided to swerve the Land Rover toward the row of adobe brick dwellings.

Then the sergeant saw the figure on the rooftop of a nearby building. Clad in army-style fatigues and a keffiyeh, complete with a face scarf that concealed his features, the man wasn't simply a lookout. He held a rocket launcher, and the warhead was pointed at the convoy of Land Rovers that rolled into the village.

"We're going straight toward him!" the NCO shouted, switching to English.

"I noticed," Bolan growled as he stomped on the sergeant's foot to push the boot hard on the accelerator.

The Executioner's actions might have seemed suicidal, but the big American warrior had instantly assessed the situation the moment he spotted the man with the RPG. They were too close to head for cover or run out of range of the Soviet-made rocket launcher. The only option was to race toward the building. The launcher was designed to be fired at long-range targets. If they could get close enough, fast enough, the ambusher might be reluctant to open fire for fear of killing himself if the rocket went off right beneath him.

Or the guy might be worried about killing some of his comrades. Bolan had no doubt there were other opponents lurking among the simple adobe structures.

The Rover bolted forward, and Bolan heard the exaggerated hiss of the RPG even as the adobe wall filled the windshield. The warrior's combat reflexes took over as he grabbed an Uzi and eased up on the gas pedal. If the enemy blasted the vehicle with the rocket, all his efforts would be for naught, but he carried them out without conscious thought. If he survived, he intended to be damn well ready to fight.

The Israeli stomped on the brake and the Rover came to a bone-jarring halt. Bolan glimpsed a stream of white smoke overhead and realized the RPG had been fired. The enemy had clearly changed his target and sent the rocket hurtling for the second Rover. The warrior leaped from the vehicle, the Uzi subgun clenched in his fist. He heard the explosion and hoped the Rover had been spared. But he couldn't afford to throw a glance over his shoulder to check it out.

The Executioner didn't look up at the man on the roof, either. He was aware the guy had fired his launcher and would have to either reload the RPG or produce another weapon. Bolan scanned the doors and windows of the dwellings. The most immediate threat was from the opponents they had yet to locate.

Sunlight flashed on a windowpane. Bolan started to raise his Uzi but detected movement from the corner of an eye. He turned swiftly and triggered the SMG, drilling an armed figure who stood on the threshold of the building. The gunman's body jerked under the impacts of 9 mm Parabellums, his AK-47 assault rifle falling to the ground as he tumbled back through the open doorway.

The sergeant swung a Galil rifle to his shoulder and sprayed a burst at the attacker with the RPG. The man on the roof screamed, then plunged forward in a graceless somersault to crash lifelessly onto the ground.

The rocket man ran out of luck, but the Israeli sergeant fared no better. Automatic gunfire from a window sliced into the man, punching him from the Land Rover and onto the sun-baked sand.

Bolan saw the Israeli go down, but kept moving. Getting himself killed wouldn't help the Israeli trooper, and it seemed apparent that the man was beyond the need for medical assistance. The warrior charged to the doorway, streams of full-auto rounds kicking up dust behind his dashing form.

The enemy obviously had the advantage of familiar territory. The longer the battle raged, the more this advantage would play on the side of the home team. The Executioner, Katz and their Israeli companions had approached the village to ask the locals for information about reports of terrorist activity in the West Bank. The place had hardly seemed sinister when only a few goats and a lone Bedouin were visible among the simple adobe huts. The appearance of the man with the RPG changed that.

They'd been looking for terrorists, and they had found them—sooner than any man in the team had expected.

Bolan crossed the threshold, Uzi first. Flame spit from the stubby barrel of the subgun as he ducked low and rushed into the room. Drab walls and crude furniture registered in his mind's eye as he scrambled for cover. The warrior glimpsed a keffiyeh-clad head snap backward, the cloth dyed red and holed by at least one Parabellum. He saw another opponent duck behind a small wooden table. Before Bolan could get off a shot he slammed into something that grunted in response.

A stocky Arab gunman had braced himself against a wall when Bolan charged into the room. He didn't realize how close Bolan was until the Executioner ran into him. The terrorist tried to raise his Russian-made PPSh-41 submachine gun. Metal clanged on metal when the frame struck Bolan's Uzi.

The warrior rammed a shoulder into the guy's chest, keeping the subgun blocked with the frame of his own

Uzi as he drove the terrorist into a corner. Bolan stomped a boot heel into his opponent's instep and slashed the Uzi across the man's temple. As the Arab started to sag against the wall, the Executioner suddenly turned, dropped to one knee and swung his Uzi toward the table. A salvo of 7.62 mm slugs slashed air above his head as the terrorist by the table opened fire.

The burst missed Bolan's skull by scant inches and smashed into the stunned terrorist in the corner. The man with the AK-47 was horrified to see his comrade's chest erupt in a column of ragged holes, was even more alarmed to see the muzzle-flash of the Uzi when the Executioner returned fire. A stream of 9 mm rounds punched the man to the floor.

Bolan inhaled deeply to try to control his pounding heart. His ears throbbed from the sound of repeated gunshots within the confined area. The room reeked with the stench of cordite and the metallic scent of fresh blood. The warrior was no stranger to these sensations and barely glanced at the bodies in the room, certain they were dead and no longer presented a threat.

The Executioner rammed a fresh clip into the well of his Uzi. He'd been at war, one way or the other, his entire adult life and learned it was best to be prepared for combat at all times. In addition to the Uzi subgun and four extra magazines Bolan also carried a Beretta 93-R in shoulder leather. Grenades, garrotes and a Kabar fighting knife were attached to his belt and harness straps.

He carried more gear than was usually necessary because the West Bank was hardly a visit to Disneyland. It had been part of Samaria and Judea in ancient times. Annexed by Jordan in 1950, the West Bank had been captured by Israel in 1967 and was still occupied by the Jewish state. Despite efforts to negotiate an independent Palestinian Arab state in the region, the West Bank remained under Israeli control and the area was the setting of constant clashes between Arabs and Jews.

Not exactly a walk in the park, Bolan thought, unless that would be New York City's Central Park around midnight. He would have armed himself in a similar manner for such a moonlight stroll, as well. The warrior dismissed such notions as he moved to the next room. He had only one problem to deal with at the moment: staying alive.

The Executioner stopped by the archway to the adjacent room. No one had emerged from this part of the dwelling, but he knew at least one man was stationed upstairs because he'd seen a figure at the window when the firefight began. The size of the building meant the stairs were located in the next room. The first floor wasn't big enough to have more than two rooms.

Bolan glanced around the bullet-riddled quarters and located a stool near the table. He scooped up the three-legged seat and tossed it through the archway. The stool clattered across the stone floor, and the warrior prepared to respond if enemy fire erupted once more.

The chatter of an assault rifle answered the lure. Bolan thrust his Uzi around the corner and saw the stool skid across the floor, propelled by a hammering of bullets that chipped wood from the legs and seat. More slugs ricocheted against stone and whined off the base of a wood-burning stove. The gunfire came from the head of a flight of brick stairs. The enemy had fired down at the stool before he realized the target wasn't alive.

Bolan didn't make the same mistake. He rushed to the side of the stairs and pointed the Uzi at the figure at the pinnacle of the steps. The guy tried to redirect the aim of his AK-47, but the Executioner triggered his SMG, directing a burst of 9 mm rounds into the terrorist's abdomen that tunneled under the rib cage to pulverize heart and lungs. The gunner's Kalashnikov slipped from his fingers as he performed a grotesque pirouette at the top of the stairs. The rifle slid down the risers, followed by the ambusher's corpse.

The American warrior yanked the pin from a fragmentation grenade and hurled the explosive orb at the head of the stairs. He fired a short burst from the Uzi to discourage anyone above from attempting to kick the grenade down the stairs. Then he ran from the kitchen, crossed the front room and returned to the entrance. The grenade exploded and the structure convulsed from the blast. Adobe cracked and part of the ceiling collapsed. Bolan stayed by the doorway,

aware the arch offered the greatest protection from the
roof if it fell in.

The terrorists in the building were history, but the
sounds of gunfire elsewhere in the village told the
warrior that the battle wasn't over.

YAKOV KATZENELENBOGEN had ordered his driver to
take cover when he spotted the man with the rocket
launcher on the roof. He gave the command in English due to the fact that it was the language he had used
most often for the past ten years as the unit commander of Phoenix Force. Katz immediately barked
a translation in rapid Hebrew.

Captain Moshin, who accompanied Katz and the
driver in the second Land Rover, urged the NCO behind the wheel to follow the other man's instructions.
The trooper didn't need extra prompting. He raced for
a low wall of adobe bricks by the perimeter of the village, reaching cover a scant moment before the rocket
struck.

The explosion blasted chunks of adobe from the
wall, which showered down onto the vehicle. The
driver groaned and slumped in his seat, blood oozing
from a scalp wound where a piece of stone had struck
hard. Katz had raised his right arm to shield his head
and face. Only the upper arm was flesh and blood.
From the elbow the limb was made of steel and plastic, with a trio of metal hooks at the end instead of a
hand.

Many men underestimated Katz. As well as being an amputee, he was middle-aged, paunchy and had iron-gray hair. Captain Moshin knew better. He'd seen Katz in action before and had witnessed the man's incredible skill and cool efficiency in combat. Indeed, Katz jumped from the Rover faster than Moshin and moved into position along the wall, an Uzi held ready. The Phoenix Force leader was almost twice as old as the captain, yet he moved with the speed and coordination of a lion.

Yet, like a lion, Katz handled short bursts of speed and strength far better than tasks requiring endurance. The years—and a fondness for pastries and Camel cigarettes—had taken a toll. Katz realized this and knew his physical limitations. He braced the Uzi subgun across his prosthesis as Moshin joined him, a Galil rifle in hand.

Katz saw Bolan leap from the first Rover and enter the nearest adobe dwelling. He also witnessed the sergeant take out the man on the roof before dying from enemy gunfire. Other rifle barrels jutted from the windows and door of another building. Enemy fire was concentrated in Bolan's direction as the Executioner's actions provided a superb distraction for Katz and the others to use to their advantage.

"Pollock has the first building covered," Katz announced, using Bolan's cover name for the mission.

"There could be half a dozen terrorists in there," Moshin declared, stunned that Katz seemed so calm about his companion taking on such odds alone.

"They shouldn't have taken on more than they could handle," the Phoenix veteran replied, confident in the Executioner's ability to prevail against multiple opponents. "Let's take care of the rest of these malevolent characters."

"Any suggestions, Colonel?" Moshin inquired. He was a veteran soldier, formerly with the Israeli Independent Paratroop Battalion, and had participated in other dangerous missions after becoming a special officer with the Mossad. Nonetheless, the captain acknowledged Katz's superior experience in such matters.

"Cover me." The older man glanced over the wall to estimate the distance to the next adobe hut. "You've got more range with that Galil than I have with my Uzi. Stay by the wall and use the cover here. When I'm in position, lob a grenade into the center of the village."

"You want a distraction," Moshin said with a nod.

"And we need it before the other side can get into position to start throwing grenades at us. They probably have them, since they're armed with automatic weapons and at least one RPG."

"What if they have more rocket launchers?" the captain inquired with consternation.

"I suppose we'll find out soon enough," Katz replied as he headed for the edge of the wall.

The one-armed warrior took a deep breath and charged, his back arched and body low. The remaining gunners were still more concerned with Bolan's position, and most didn't even notice Katz approach. Moshin saw two gun barrels move toward the Phoenix Force pro and fired his Galil at the would-be snipers. Bullets chipped adobe from their shelter, and one rifle barrel vanished from view. Moshin didn't know whether he had hit the gunman.

An Arab assassin, armed with a French MAT submachine gun, leaned around a door to return fire at Moshin's position. He suddenly spotted Katz closing in and swung his chattergun in the commando's direction.

The Uzi fired first. The familiar recoil rode up Katz's left hand and arm and vibrated against his prosthesis to the stump of his other arm. The guy at the doorway stumbled away from the threshold and triggered his MAT blaster. The shots went wild as his body turned slightly and wilted to the ground. Katz had drilled the guy with two Parabellums in the heart, but the man had tried to resist death until his life pump convinced him it was all over.

Katz darted to the side of the building and narrowly avoided a stream of sizzling 7.62 mm slugs from an enemy AK-47. The shelter wasn't large because the adobe hut was only half the size of the two-story structure Bolan had hit. Katz's cover didn't allow much room to move and left him vulnerable to a cross fire if the enemy decided to strike from both ends of the dwelling simultaneously. However, the smaller building also meant there were fewer opponents inside to deal with.

Moshin hurled a hand grenade across the wall and sent the egg-shaped package into the clearing at the center of the village. It exploded with a deafening roar and sprayed sand and pebbles in all directions. Katz hoped the diversion convinced the terrorists to stay behind cover as he moved to the single entrance of the hut and tossed an M-26 fragger through the portal.

Katz rushed around the corner of the building and threw himself to the ground, covered his head with his artificial arm and pressed his body against the base of the wall. The grenade exploded within the dwelling, chunks of adobe bursting from the walls and rooftop. Fragments and stone dust pelted Katz's prone form. This was a small discomfort, but he was aware no one inside the structure could have survived when the grenade exploded.

A furious barrage of full-auto fire snarled from the doorway of another hut. Bullets tore into the wall at the village limits and forced Captain Moshin to stay low. Slugs chipped brick and pounded the wall with mechanical efficiency. The terrorists had set up a light machine gun at the door and used it to pin down Moshin. The steady wave of high-velocity rounds also kept Katz from moving from his position. The enemy had both men trapped and could easily take them out if they could get close enough to lob grenades or establish a cross-fire fork attack.

Bolan discovered his companions were in trouble and quickly evaluated the situation. The machine gun nest at the threshold to one dwelling didn't seem to be in danger of running out of ammo while four men, armed with Kalashnikovs and grenades, advanced from the remaining hut. The tide of battle had switched dramatically in favor of the terrorists.

The warrior glanced down at the corpse of the man who had been shot off the rooftop. The RPG launcher lay near the corpse. He'd managed to load another rocket into the weapon before he was killed. Bolan scooped up the RPG and made certain the warhead was in place. The Executioner realized the launcher might have been damaged when it fell to the ground, and there was a possibility the weapon would misfire or even blow up in Bolan's hands.

He couldn't waste time checking it out. The lives of Katz and Moshin depended on swift action, and Bolan responded accordingly. He raised the RPG, quickly aimed at the machine gun nest and triggered the weapon. The rocket burst from the muzzle and streaked across the village. The warhead scored a direct hit in the center of the doorway. The explosion blasted the machine gun and crew into oblivion. Metal and human remains mingled with jagged pieces of adobe as the hut blew apart. The force of the blast spread across the hamlet and knocked two enemy gunners off their feet.

The other pair of terrorists dropped to the ground when the explosion occurred. Their attention turned from Katz and Moshin to see what happened to their comrades. The gunmen saw Bolan discard the RPG and advance, Uzi up and ready. One man pointed his

AK-47 at the Executioner, but Bolan triggered his SMG before the terrorist could open fire. The burst of 9 mm slugs drilled into the gunman's forehead.

His companion rolled away from the bullet-ravaged body of the slain terrorist. The guy tried to aim his Kalashnikov at Bolan while seeking shelter. He failed at both efforts when Katz stepped from cover and fired his Uzi. The terrorist absorbed a trio of Parabellums that split his spinal cord and punctured his liver. His body performed a brief death spasm, then dropped to the blood-smeared ground.

Bolan approached the two terrorists who had been knocked down by the concussion of the rocket explosion. Katz called to Moshin in Hebrew and told the captain to hold his fire. Moshin understood English, but Katz still addressed the Israeli agent in his native language to be certain Moshin comprehended the message in a high-stress situation. Katz covered Bolan as the Executioner knelt by the fallen terrorists.

"This one's alive," the warrior announced when he found a pulse in the side of the first man's neck.

There was no need to check the second terrorist for vital signs. A shard of metal from the smashed machine gun had hit the guy in the back of the neck. Six inches of steel jutted from the base of his skull. The rocket blast had turned the metal splinter into a giant dart, propelled with bulletlike velocity. The terrorist had been pinned with lethal results.

"Good," Katz remarked as he watched Bolan frisk the guy for weapons. "Hopefully he can answer a few questions for us."

"Do you think these are the men who kidnapped Birnbaum's people?" Moshin inquired as he climbed over the wall to join Bolan and Katz.

"I don't know," the Executioner replied bluntly. "They tried to kill us and that's a good enough reason to take them down. Let's check out what's left of this place and take the prisoner back to the base. We'll have a better idea what's going on then. Right now we've got more questions and no answers."

MACK BOLAN WAITED patiently for Katz's return, filling in the time by cleaning and oiling a disassembled M-16. The veteran of a thousand campaigns, from the so-called "police action" in Southeast Asia to his incredible one-man war against crime, Bolan had learned to make the most of any lull during a mission. Katz spoke fluent Arabic, thus fell to him the job of interrogating the lone Arab survivor of the terrorist ambush. Since Bolan didn't share Katz's linguistic skill, he busied himself with his gear while waiting for news of the inquisition.

He sat on a bench in a corridor of the catacombs where the Mossad had established a temporary base for the mission. The site was centuries old and located between Jerusalem and Moza Illit. The tunnels and subterranean chambers had been built during the Roman occupation of Israel. However, it had limited interest to archaeologists because the catacombs had been used for underground dwellings and bunkers from the first Arab conquests of 636 A.D. to the Six Day War in 1967. Ancient artifacts had long ago been removed, and the catacombs had little historic significance because they weren't especially unique. Hundreds of tunnels, aqueducts and catacombs were located throughout the country.

The Mossad had chosen the site because it was obscure and known to relatively few people. The catacombs offered excellent security and total privacy for Bolan and the men assigned to his mission. It wasn't the most comfortable safe house the Executioner had encountered, but he'd seen far worse.

He examined the M-16 under the harsh light of a naked bulb. The assault rifle was part of the "special package" sent in by diplomatic pouch to the U.S. embassy. Bolan was satisfied with the weapon and reassembled it. An M-203 grenade launcher was attached to the underside of the barrel like an oversize front stock. The Executioner had used this lethal combination many times in the past. He'd been supplied with spare magazines, two thousand rounds of 5.56 mm ammunition and thirty 40 mm cartridge-style grenades for the launcher.

The Mossad had also provided him with a .44 Magnum Desert Eagle. The powerful handgun was manufactured by Israel Military Industries, so the Mossad had little trouble getting an Eagle for the Executioner. The weapon consisted of only five main parts, and Bolan easily fieldstripped and examined the pistol for a fundamental inspection. The big .44 was fit for duty, and the warrior added it to his arsenal. Accessories for the Eagle included a combat hip holster, three extra magazines and three hundred .44 Magnum shells.

Katz and Captain Moshin finally appeared from the chamber where the prisoner was temporarily confined. Their expressions told the Executioner that the interrogation had produced little information. He didn't expect good news when Yakov spoke.

"Our guest was talkative," the Phoenix commander announced. "He threatened, cursed, bragged and demanded throughout the interrogation. Unfortunately he didn't confess to kidnapping any members of the Samson Warriors or having anything to do with the bombing at the hotel in Tel Aviv."

"I don't have to tell you terrorists aren't necessarily the most truthful people you'll meet," Bolan reminded Katz. "He might be lying."

"He'll be questioned again under the influence of scopolamine," Moshin declared. "We have to move him to a clinical setting and have this done by experts in the use of truth serum. Scopolamine can be lethal if the dose is too strong."

"That might get some additional information from the man," Katz commented, "but I doubt it will be useful to us. Our captive claims he and his deceased friends belong to the Palestinian Islamic Liberation Army.''

''Maybe I'm supposed to know the names of all these fanatic outfits in the Middle East,'' Bolan began, ''but I have to admit I never heard of this one before. Is it major league or just a splinter group?''

''Definitely minor,'' Moshin answered. ''The PILA is trying to emulate the old Black September terrorists of the seventies, but it's much smaller and not as well trained. Not well organized and only marginally associated with any of the main Palestinian groups, they've conducted violent actions against Israeli troops in the West Bank and Gaza Strip for the past few months.''

''Our prisoner says that's why they attacked us,'' Katz added. ''He claims they saw us coming in the Land Rovers, noticed the drivers were dressed in Israeli army uniforms and prepared to take us out. The terrorists had only recently acquired their military hardware and used it to drive out local residents and take over the village as a regional base. We simply arrived at the right time to be a target.''

''You believe him?'' Bolan asked.

''Unless the truth serum proves the man is a far more gifted liar than I think he is,'' Katz said with a nod. ''When I asked him about Birnbaum and the Samson Warriors, his expression didn't betray any sign that he knew what I was talking about. He bragged about other actions by the PILA and probably would have taken credit for the bombing at Tel Aviv if he had known about it.''

''I'm afraid we encountered the wrong group of terrorists,'' Moshin remarked. ''Of course, I'm rather glad they've been taken out of action because they were still a threat to Israelis in the region.''

The news didn't surprise Bolan, and he didn't expect the mission to be completed so quickly. ''Let's check out Birnbaum and his cronies.''

''You think it more likely the Samson Warriors staged the incidents at the hotel than the sabotage was the work of Palestinian fanatics?'' Moshin asked. The Mossad agent's tone suggested he would rather be stalking Arab than Jewish suspects.

''We looked into the claims of a terrorist kidnapping and activity in the West Bank,'' Bolan replied. ''The lead didn't pan out aside from the gang of half-wits we came across today. Birnbaum and the Samson Warriors have criminal records back in the States. They have histories of violence and political extremism. I wouldn't say I'm more suspicious of them than the possibility that Palestinian terrorists are involved, but I sure can't write them off the list of suspects.''

''Neither has the Mossad,'' Moshin assured him. ''We've been keeping track of their activities since the bombing occurred.''

"You mentioned that Birnbaum is having a rally of some sort in Tel Aviv later today," Katz reminded the captain.

"Yes. We've arranged something concerning it, as well. Perhaps you'd like to attend and see Mr. Birnbaum in person."

"Yeah," Bolan said. "I'd like to get a look at the guy."

3

Levi Birnbaum stood on a platform and addressed the crowd of angry Israelis. The media was present, which was fine with the leader of the Samson Warriors. International reporters and Israeli television and newspaper people were scattered throughout the crowd. Birnbaum was a charismatic figure. His powerful physique was displayed in khaki and combat boots, and he looked like a soldier in spite of the absence of rank or military decorations.

His American comrades were there, minus the five men who vanished from the hotel and Ezra Avriel. The American media had learned about Ezra's past. The negative publicity associated with Ezra didn't help the Samson Warriors' image. It was bad enough the press had discovered that Avriel spent three years in a mental hospital for assaulting several women. Birnbaum didn't want the man present to remind the reporters that a certified lunatic was among the ranks.

No matter. Ezra was better suited to tasks carried out in the shadows. The man had skills that were useful despite his unbalanced psyche. As long as Avriel was kept on a leash, his talents compensated for the liabilities of having him on Birnbaum's team.

"How much longer are Jews to be victims?" Birnbaum demanded as he fixed the crowd with his fierce dark eyes. "Wasn't the State of Israel established to protect Jews? Isn't this supposed to be our haven? A place of safety and shelter where all the sons and daughters of Abraham can live in peace?"

Birnbaum shook his head in an exaggerated gesture for the sake of the spectators and TV cameras. Theater was part of his success. He had trained his voice and studied body language to be an effective public speaker. His personality and performances were the foundation of the Samson Warriors and the primary method of recruiting new members.

"That is the dream!" he announced in a loud, hard voice. "But we see the reality. We saw how safe Jews are right here in Tel Aviv when a PLO bomb murdered innocent guests at the Rishon Hotel. Arab terrorists abducted five of my closest comrades and friends. What sort of men commit such ruthless and brutal acts? Cowards who are afraid of a strong Israel and fear the Samson Warriors because we stand for an Israel that will be feared and respected by the entire world." He allowed a dramatic pause and added, "Especially by the Arab world."

Birnbaum repeated his remarks in Hebrew for the sake of the Israelis who didn't understand English. He also wanted to avoid having his words interpreted by the IBA for Israeli radio and television because too much could be altered or misunderstood through translation.

He was particularly interested in delivering his message to the groups of young Israelis in the congregation. Some who attended the rally were teenagers. When the males reached eighteen, they would be required to serve a mandatory term in the military. Some females would also be called upon to serve. These young people had good reason to wonder about the future of Israel and what would be asked of them due to government policies.

A few men in the crowd were dressed in army uniform, and others were probably military personnel clad in civilian clothes. However, not all those present attended because they admired Birnbaum and the Samson Warriors. He knew some of the figures in uniform were police and military assigned to keep order and perhaps to protect the people at the rally.

No doubt there were government agents among the crowd, as well, Birnbaum realized. The Mossad would certainly have someone there to observe the proceedings. The CIA would be represented, too, and perhaps other intelligence agencies of other nations had eyes and ears at the meeting.

He noticed two men at the perimeter of the crowd. One was tall and dark, his companion older with gray hair and a few inches shorter. Birnbaum wasn't sure why the pair made a special impression, but he sensed they weren't casual observers. They wore loose-fitting jackets in spite of the heat, and he suspected this might be to conceal weapons hidden beneath the garments.

The big man especially caught his eye. Although the guy's clothes concealed most of his physique, and members of the crowd further blocked Birnbaum's view of the stranger, the Samson leader guessed the man was an athlete. His expression was serious, and he didn't appear to be a journalist. And the guy looked hard.

As long as the man didn't cause any problems, Birnbaum didn't care if the stranger was nasty enough to strangle a grizzly bear with one hand. If he became trouble, Birnbaum was confident his men could deal with the guy regardless of how tough he might be.

"How can Jews ever expect to be safe if we cannot be secure within the heart of Israel?" Birnbaum continued. "The Jewish state can never be truly secure until we are so strong no one dares to oppose us."

He quickly repeated the statements in Hebrew and thrust both arms into the air. Birnbaum's thick biceps strained the fabric of the khaki shirt sleeves. His barrel chest appeared ready to pop the buttons as he flexed powerful pectoral muscles.

"Although I was born in the United States, I say *we!*" Birnbaum declared in a bellowing voice. "I am a Jew! I am an Israeli! This is my country, and I want it to be strong and independent of other nations. Don't rely on American support for Israel. The United States has lost interest in our country and regards Israel as a burden and an unruly bully in the Middle East. Don't rely on the United Nations. Look how Israel was condemned during the *intifadeh*."

The Samson leader punched the air as if fighting an invisible opponent as he declared, "Israel cannot rely on anyone except itself! We must be independent and we must be secure. I want the enemies of Israel to be the ones who tremble with fear! It would be better that Israel destroy itself in a war against the Arab nations than become a quivering pup surrounded by blood-thirsty hounds!"

The American Samson Warriors began to cheer. Others in the crowd joined them. Birnbaum translated his remarks, and more Israelis added their applause. He was saying what the frustrated and angry audience members wanted to hear, Bolan observed. Israel tended to be thin-skinned about criticism about the *intifadeh* and worried about U.S.-Israeli relations.

The Jewish state was also concerned about hostility by Arab nations. Israel had survived several wars with its neighbors. The aggressive actions by Syria, Libya and especially Iraq gave Israel plenty of reason to worry. When Iraq invaded Kuwait, Saddam Hussein had become a hero to many Arabs by complaining that Israel had occupied the West Bank for years without criticism from America, let alone with the U.S. responding with troops. Israeli-hating Arabs in many countries were willing to sign recruiting papers to join the Iraqi army.

Although the Arab nations at the Cairo conference had condemned Saddam's actions, Iraq's anti-Israel propaganda had a lot of people worried. The vast majority of Arabs would never support a man like Hussein in a holy war against the United States and Israel, but the tension in the Middle East had escalated with every passing day. Israel had good reason to believe it would have no allies if one or more of its Arab neighbors decided to attack.

Birnbaum appreciated the fear and anger that simmered within many Israelis. This was especially true about many young Israelis who wondered what sort of world they would inherit. Without U.S. aid the Israeli economy would fall apart. The country suffered crushing inflation, and it was surrounded by enemies. Israel might be paranoid, but it had reason to be.

"The Samson Warriors were created to fight the enemies of Israel," Birnbaum declared. "Samson was God's instrument of justice on earth. With strength given him by God Samson slew a thousand Philistines with only the jawbone of an ass. With God behind us Israel will defeat any enemy, regardless of the odds, as long as our nation remains strong and becomes stronger."

The Executioner glanced at Katz. The older man's expression didn't hint as to what he was thinking, but Bolan knew the Phoenix Force commander well enough to guess that he was disgusted by Birnbaum's actions. Katz was an intellectual and a scholar, a master linguist and lifetime student of culture and history. He had formerly served the Israeli government and still believed in what the Jewish state stood for. Birnbaum's twisted version of this dream was surely offensive to Katz.

"Seen enough?" Bolan asked.

"Enough to need some aspirin," Katz replied with a nod.

They left the rally and waved down a passing cab. Tel Aviv was a modern city. Bolan noticed high-rise apartment buildings, office towers and new projects under construction as the vehicle traveled through the bustling streets. They passed Bet Dizengoff or Bible Museum and the Shalom Tower. The Great Synagogue and the Haganah Museum, noted for its collection of memorabilia of Israel's struggle for independence, were also visible from the taxi windows.

However, the huge white dome of the Hassan Bek Mosque, in view in the distance, was evidence that Judaism wasn't the only religion represented in Tel Aviv. Many churches and mosques were located in the city. Although Israel was a "Jewish state," it was also a parliamentary democracy and placed no restrictions on other religions. Christians and Muslims were free to practice their beliefs and attend the house of worship of their choice.

However, Israel was a long way from utopia. Accusations of violations of human rights by the Israeli government and military had increased since the start of the *intifadeh*. The term referred to the violent confrontations between Israeli troops and Arabs living in the West Bank and Gaza Strip. Hundreds of young Arab protestors, opposed to Israeli occupation of land that had formerly been Arab territory, had been killed by soldiers. Government policies included evacuating Arab families from their homes and blowing up the buildings. There were also persistent stories that some soldiers had tortured Arabs suspected of being PLO collaborators.

Aside from internal unrest and the constant threat of war with its neighbors in the Middle East, Israel was also plagued with economic woes. Most Israelis paid more than seventy percent of their annual income in taxes, largely to support the military. This was especially frustrating for Israelis because they realized their country was dependent on foreign aid from the United States in spite of the heavy tax burden.

Bolan considered these facts as the cab rolled to a stop at the curb in front of a restaurant. Israel's vast assortment of problems made it vulnerable in many ways. Birnbaum and the Samson Warriors were trying to exploit the anger, fear and frustrations of Israelis. However, this didn't prove that the American-bred extremists were ruthless enough to kill innocent people to make a fake kidnapping more convincing...*if* the abduction of the five missing members was faked. Birnbaum's radical rhetoric could have caused Palestinian terrorists to target the Samson Warriors for a hit.

Running around in circles, the Executioner thought as he stepped from the cab. This wasn't the sort of mission he generally dealt with. He usually had a clear target and could tell friend from foe without having to work for the information. Perhaps this was a reflection of the way the world had changed. It had become steadily more difficult to distinguish allies and enemies on every level.

Katz paid the cabdriver and the two men entered the restaurant. Captain Moshin was waiting for them at a table in a corner of the room. The Israeli officer looked different dressed in civilian clothing, seemed younger without the uniform. Perhaps because the burden of command was briefly lifted from his shoulders, in appearance if not in reality.

The Stony Man warriors joined Moshin. A waiter approached the table and addressed them in Hebrew, which was immediately followed by an English translation. They ordered meals and waited for the first round of coffee. When the waiter left the table, Moshin opened a briefcase and removed a pair of large brown envelopes. He handed one to Bolan.

"You'll find the names, photographs and descriptions of the five Samson Warriors who were allegedly abducted from the Rishon Hotel," Moshin explained. "Birnbaum supplied the pictures and most of the other information."

"We can compare the photos with their mug shots," Bolan commented. "We can also check the files we brought on the Samsons' criminal records and find out what sort of ex-convicts we're looking for."

"Your friends in Washington sent us that information by fax machine," Moshin told him. "The Mossad might be able to convince our immigration ministry to deny citizenship to some of the Samson Warriors or even deport them as undesirables. Most of their criminal records aren't serious enough to merit such actions. We also contacted Interpol to see if any of them were wanted for crimes at an international level."

"Could have saved you the trouble," Bolan stated. "Our people already ran a check with Interpol through the Justice Department back in the States."

"The American branch of Interpol is attached to the Justice Department," Katz explained for Moshin's benefit. "Whatever else Birnbaum and his followers have done, they haven't appeared on any Interpol lists. Not yet at least."

"What did you think of the rally?" the captain inquired.

"Birnbaum is a rabble-rouser," Bolan answered. "Potentially dangerous if he can convince followers to agree to radical actions as violent as those he appears to advocate."

"Appears to advocate?" Moshin asked with surprise. "I thought Birnbaum was rather direct in his statements."

"Yeah," Bolan said, "but he might water that down a bit if he starts getting more followers. A lot of firebrands cool off when their political groups become larger. Afraid they might have to deliver some of their promises or that the host government is going to start taking them more seriously. Birnbaum might be that type."

"Or he might be as fanatical as he seems," Katz added.

"That's possible, too," the big warrior agreed. "Any luck on grilling the Arab gunman we caught earlier today? Last we heard the Mossad was going to interrogate him with drugs."

"The prisoner was given scopolamine," Moshin confirmed. "Unfortunately his story didn't change. The man is indeed a member of the PILA terrorist organization. He's probably residing in a prison cell now. I can speak for all of the Mossad and the Israeli military when I say we're all glad he's behind bars. None of us will be shedding any tears over the graves of his slain comrades, either."

"Be that as it may, Captain," Bolan said as he sipped some coffee, "those men attacked us simply because we were in the wrong place at the wrong time. They had nothing to do with the hotel bombing or the Samson Warriors."

"And nothing to do with our mission," Katz added, taking a pack of Camels from his pocket.

"We'll know about Birnbaum and the Samsons in the very near future," Moshin assured his companions. "One of my men, Lieutenant Daniel Yarok, was also at the rally today. He was at one yesterday, and he'll keep attending until they trust him enough to accept him as a new recruit.''

"He's pretending to be an eager young zealot among the civilian population?'' Katz asked with a frown. He fired a cigarette with his lighter and shook his head. "That's very risky. If he infiltrates the Samsons, he'll have to be careful. Extremists are paranoid by nature. It's hard to say what they might do if they suspect Yarok is a spy.''

"He's a very good man,'' Moshin insisted. "Yarok volunteered for the assignment. He knows the risks involved.''

"No, he doesn't,'' the Executioner corrected. "None of us knows what the Samson Warriors are doing here or just what they might be capable of.''

4

Afif Rifai was tired. She always felt tired. Seventy years old, the woman figured she had a right to be tired. She'd been born in Palestine when the British still occupied the country. Her father had fought the Turks and supported the British because England had promised the Arabs that Palestine would be an independent state after the war.

However, Jewish immigration to Palestine had steadily increased, and the British tried to accommodate Jews and Arabs without pleasing either side. England restricted Jewish immigration into Palestine in the late 1930s, but conflicts and violence between Arabs and Jews were already dividing the country.

After World War II and the Holocaust, international sympathy for the Jewish struggle for an independent state convinced the British to turn over the Palestine issue to the UN in 1947. Palestinian Arabs clashed with Jewish settlers. The former far outnumbered the latter, but the Jewish forces were better organized and prepared for war. The Haganah was well trained and well armed. The Palestinian forces were fragmented, and most of the Arab leaders were in exile.

Afif recalled the terrible war that followed. Both Jews and Palestinians resorted to acts of terrorism. Atrocities were committed by both sides. In less than a year the Palestinians were defeated, and nearly eight hundred thousand Palestinian refugees were forced out to make room for the growing number of Jewish immigrants who continued to flood into the new nation of Israel. Yet Afif and what remained of her family stayed in the Arab sections.

She'd been forced to move many times and eventually went to live in the West Bank. The years had been hard for the woman. Her husband had died twenty years earlier and her children were grown with families of their own. Her grandchildren were her greatest joy, but she seldom saw them. She usually spent her time at the loom or cleaning her two-room home.

Afif sat on a stool outside her home, weaving at the loom and watching children play among the other houses in the village. The sight pleased her because she loved children, but they also reminded her of her own son, daughters and grandchildren, which made her miss her family more than usual. She also recalled her own childhood and raising children during the conflicts that plagued the region since Israel was established in 1948. Growing up had been hard, and it seemed unlikely it would be easier for the new generation.

She tried not to think about such things. Events had occurred in her lifetime that she had been unable to deal with in any manner other than simply accepting what fate dealt to her.

As Afif tugged the cowl of her head scarf forward to protect her eyes from the afternoon sun, three young men walked from their homes. They were dressed in white shirts and American-style pants and sneakers. The old woman had once objected to Arabs dressing in a manner she considered "European," but this now seemed a minor issue compared to the more serious problems facing the Middle East. The youths were students at a university and hoped to earn degrees in engineering and architecture. They hoped to improve their standard of living in the future. Perhaps, Afif thought hopefully, some changes could be for the better.

The eruption of automatic weapons came without warning. The old woman was horror-struck as she watched bullet holes pop across the chests of the young students, crimson staining their white shirts as the trio staggered from the impacts of the high-velocity slugs. Their books fell from their hands, and the men tumbled to the ground as another wave of bullets ripped into their flesh.

Afif turned toward the source of the gunshots. Half a dozen men had entered the village, faces and heads concealed by masks of rubber and plastic. They were dressed in Israeli army uniforms, and two of the soldiers continued to fire Galil rifles at the fallen students, butchering their bodies.

Mothers shouted to the children, fearful of their safety. Men and women emerged from their homes, pleading with the soldiers not to open fire on the children. One of the masked figures promptly swung his rifle at the civilians and triggered the weapon.

Bullets tore into male and female victims without discrimination. Bodies fell to the ground, screaming and thrashing around in agony. Survivors raced for cover in time to avoid the volley of rounds that followed. Afif was relieved to see that the children had found shelter inside a house that hadn't come under attack by the demented soldiers, but the six assassins continued to fire on the village in the senseless and brutal assault.

Afif had watched the carnage with such disbelief and horror that she had forgotten to seek safety. When a soldier turned his Uzi on her, she stared at the muzzle and saw flame burst from the barrel. Half a dozen Parabellum rounds drilled into the woman and flung her onto the loom. She felt little pain because the massive shock of the bullets obliterated nerve centers. She realized all her disappointments and suffering had come to an end. Afif was no longer tired as the final flickering of her life vanished.

SAUL ROSEN and Sharon Helms knelt by an adobe brick wall at the edge of the village. Free-lance reporters, they'd come to Israel in search of a big story that would open the door to careers with a major TV network back in the States. The couple had pooled their financial resources to afford the trip to the Middle East. It had been a big gamble, but one that had suddenly paid off.

The West Bank seemed an ideal spot to try to shoot some scenes of the troubled region and interview Arabs and Jews about the *intifadeh*. The couple was astonished to witness the vicious, unprovoked attack on the small Arab hamlet. Rosen was especially stunned and revolted by the scene. Although he tried to remain objective as a television journalist, he'd hoped to be able to present Israel in a favorable light. He didn't want to believe Jews could be capable of such actions.

Yet he'd seen the assault with his own eyes.

"Saul," Sharon rasped, moving the video camera on her shoulder as she spoke, "look over there!"

He gazed at a group of young Arab males gathered between two buildings at the opposite end of the village. They donned hood masks and wrapped checked keffiyehs across their faces. Sharon adjusted the long-range lens as she focused her view on the youths. They carried an assortment of weapons that included bottles with rags jammed into the top of the glass necks, and leather slings. Three men had handguns, old revolvers with worn metal finish and spots of rust on the frames and barrels.

"My God," Rosen whispered, his voice barely audible and choked with emotion. "There's going to be more killing."

"We're here to cover the news," Sharon reminded him. She'd always been more dedicated to pure journalism than Saul, and she had no emotional ties to Israel. "This is one hell of a story and we're not going to blow it, Saul."

Rosen wasn't surprised at her lack of caring. Sharon didn't know what it meant to be a Jew. He hadn't practiced his religion much since he reached adulthood, but he still felt an admiration for Israel.

The Jewish state was David surrounded by Arab Goliaths. They were the brave Hebrew warriors who reclaimed their homeland and created a country where Jews could be strong and free. Yet Rosen had never seen Israeli troops as gun-toting storm troopers until that day. How was this possible? These were the children of the Holocaust survivors. How could they behave in this manner?

Sharon swung the camera back to the gunmen clad in Israeli uniforms and gas masks. The headgear made them resemble giant insects that walked upright, the bug-eye lenses and plastic filters robbing them of human features. The killers could have been alien invaders from another planet. Perhaps it would be less appalling if they had been Martians rather than human assassins who butchered other human beings without a trace of hesitation or compassion.

"They're leaving," Sharon announced as she watched the hit team retreat from the village. "Maybe they know the Arab kids are getting ready to fight back."

"Cowards as well as killers," Rosen replied, nearly in tears from the shattering experience.

The sound of engines drew their attention to the road alongside the village. Military trucks had arrived and Israeli soldiers jumped from the vehicles, weapons in hand. They wore helmets instead of gas masks and several men carried large shields made of metal and Plexiglas. Many had riot batons as well as firearms.

Palestinian rebels appeared among the bullet-scarred buildings. Two hooded figures swung slings overhead, leather thongs clenched in angry fists. They unleashed their missiles, and the stones hurtled among the Israeli troops. One rock bounced against a riot shield. The other struck a soldier in the chest and knocked him to the ground.

Masked Arabs opened fire with pistols while another rebel lobbed a Molotov cocktail at the transport trucks. The bottle burst on the pavement, and gasoline ignited from the flaming rag fuse. Fire erupted among the troops. An Israeli screamed as his fatigue pants caught fire and his leg burned with the cloth. The blaze extended to the canvas tarp of a truck and began to spread across the vehicle.

The pistol shots and another volley of sling stones forced the Israelis to seek cover. Two soldiers rushed to the burning trooper and smothered the flames. Another managed to use a fire extinguisher to spray the truck with foam and put out the blaze that threatened the rig. He cried out when a rebel bullet punched into his stomach.

The soldiers opened fire. A sling-wielding figure tumbled to the ground, his chest riddled by 5.56 mm slugs. One of his companions prepared to lob a gas bomb, but he, too, was shot dead before the missile was airborne. The guy fell behind the cover of an adobe dwelling, and the bottle of gasoline exploded to engulf the wounded man and a comrade with flames.

Screams echoed within the village as Israelis and Arabs played a lethal version of hide-and-seek. Tear gas grenades were thrown by the soldiers, but the Palestinians' masks and hoods helped protect them from the fumes. However, the tide of battle soon shifted in favor of the well-armed and well-trained Israelis.

"Bo haina!" a soldier shouted, pointing an Uzi submachine gun at Saul and Sharon.

"Oh, shit," Sharon rasped, even as she swung the video camera at the approaching Israeli.

"What do they want?" Rosen wondered aloud as he raised his trembling hands.

"You're asking me?" Sharon replied, still filming the soldiers. "You're Jewish. Didn't they teach you any Hebrew when you were growing up?"

"I know a little Yiddish. Mostly rude remarks that aren't going to get us anywhere."

"Bo haina!" the trooper repeated, but he raised the Uzi to avoid threatening the pair with the subgun.

A young officer stepped forward and translated the command. "Come here, please. We must take you into protective custody and ask you a few questions."

"Up yours," Sharon replied, but she didn't speak loud enough to be heard by the soldiers.

"Don't mess with these guys," Rosen urged. "They aren't playing around."

"And please give me the camera, ma'am," the officer requested, his tone polite yet firm.

"Like hell!" she snapped, more angry than frightened. "You can't suppress the news! We're Americans, mister..."

"That must be very nice for you," the officer said with a smile. "Now give me the camera and come along quietly."

5

Captain Moshin pressed the play button on the video tape recorder. The images of the carnage at the Arab village appeared on a TV screen. Bolan and Katz watched the masked figures in Israeli uniforms open fire on the unarmed civilians. The footage was occasionally jerky due to the movement of Sharon Helms's video camera, but there was no doubt the attack had been unprovoked. The Palestinian rebels didn't enter the battle until the slaughter was over.

"This is terrible," Katz said, shaking his head sadly. "You say the journalists just happened to be in the area? No one tipped them in advance?"

"That's what they say," Moshin confirmed. "The Mossad is holding them for questioning, but we can't do it for long. They're American citizens, and they didn't break any laws by being in the West Bank. Needless to say, they're already asking to contact the U.S. embassy and demanding the return of their videotape."

"I'm not surprised," Bolan commented. "This is a big story on the *intifadeh*. I'm also sure the Mossad won't return the tape."

"Not until we've run a magnet over it and erased the contents by 'accident,'" Moshin admitted. "Israel has gotten enough bad press from the American media. We'd be fools to release something that so clearly damns the Israeli military as the aggressors in the *intifadeh* conflict."

"The unit commander of the patrol that arrives here spoke with you?" Katz asked, still watching the TV screen. The Israelis in the trucks had appeared on the videotape.

"Yes. He insists none of his men were in the area until they responded to the sounds of gunshots. He stated that they heard the reports of automatic weapons, although he admits that none of the Palestinians they encountered were armed with any firearms aside from the revolvers. Very old revolvers at that. Two were 9 mm Parabellum versions of American Smith & Wesson service revolvers that were produced in the mid-1960s. The other gun was a British Enfield revolver that was a relic from the pre-Independence time."

"Rewind the tape," Bolan instructed. "I want to see it again."

"I don't think this has anything to do with your mission here, Mr. Pollock," Moshin said as he approached the VCR. "Unfortunately I'm afraid we have a group of Israeli troops playing vigilante. I just hope we can find these men and make them pay for this atrocity."

"Unfortunately Israeli soldiers have resorted to brutality and excessive force in the past," Katz added for Bolan's sake, unsure how familiar the Executioner was with the history of the *intifadeh.* "To its credit, however, Israel has court-martialed more than a dozen soldiers for such behavior."

"And we'll court-martial half a dozen more," Moshin added. "This sort of abuse cannot be tolerated. The fact they were Israeli military makes their conduct even more inexcusable."

"I still want to see the tape again."

The news of the violence in the West Bank had been waiting for them when they returned from Tel Aviv. Mossad Director Geller had agreed to allow the men to enter the headquarters building in Jerusalem to view the videotape and interrogate the people connected with the incident.

Bolan and Katz left the latter task of the Mossad. They didn't want to jeopardize their own security for the mission. The results of the clash between Israelis and Arabs at the village were alarming even by *intifadeh* standards. Two Israeli soldiers and fifteen Arabs had been killed. Seven other soldiers and twenty Arabs were injured, some seriously. About half the Arab casualties had been armed Palestinian rebels, but the others were innocent Arab villagers.

A hell of a mess, Bolan thought as he sat in the Mossad briefing room and watched the images on the TV screen.

"You think this incident is somehow connected with your mission here?" Moshin asked.

"I don't know yet," the Executioner replied, "but the attack on the village by the original group of men in uniforms is pretty strange. These six guys are wearing protective gas masks, but they didn't use tear gas. None of them are even carrying grenades."

"You're right," Katz agreed. "No tear gas was used until the troops arrived in the trucks and fought the masked Palestinians."

"So they wore the masks to hide their faces," Moshin mused. "Did they know the journalists were in the West Bank?"

"Maybe," Bolan answered, "but they damn sure knew the Israeli patrol was in the area. They might have even known about the Palestinian rebels in the village. By shooting up the place they set the gears in motion for the soldiers and the rebels to confront one another. Doesn't take a genius to realize the soldiers would rush to the area when they heard gunshots or the rebels would arm themselves and come out of their corner ready to take on any Israeli they laid eyes on."

"And they were trying to hide their identity from *anyone* who might see them," Katz added.

"Yeah," Bolan confirmed as he pointed at the killers on the screen. "Take a better look at those uniforms. No unit crests, no name tags, no rank insignia.

The weapons are Israeli manufacture, and their uniforms and boots appear to be the same style worn by the IDF troops, but that doesn't mean they're Israeli soldiers."

"If they're not renegade soldiers," Moshin began in a puzzled tone, "who are they? I wouldn't reject the possibility of the PLO and some of the other Palestinian extremists being capable of any sort of terrible act. Nonetheless, this would be an extraordinary stunt even for them."

"It's hard to imagine that the PLO or any other Palestinian 'resistance' group would slaughter Arab civilians and set up some of their own supporters to fight a very one-sided battle with Israeli troops as part of a propaganda effort to make the Israeli military look bad," Katz commented. "That's pretty far-fetched, although I wouldn't say it's impossible."

"A large number of Arabs in the West Bank and Gaza Strip have been beaten and murdered by Palestinian fanatics who accused them of cooperating with Israeli authorities," Moshin stated. "Don't be so sure the PLO or someone like them isn't responsible."

"I guess you can't dismiss that possibility," Bolan said as he watched the killers on the screen vanish from view. "But it seems as unlikely as a gang of renegade Israeli troops. That's another possibility that has to be considered. There's also a third group that could have done this. Somebody who isn't with the Israeli military or the Palestinians."

"The Samson Warriors?" Moshin said with a frown.

"We know they're radicals and were capable of crimes of violence in the past," the Executioner reminded the Mossad officer. "They advocate aggressive action by Israel, and Birnbaum preaches extreme offense as Israel's best form of national defense."

"But are they ruthless enough to slaughter innocent people in the village?" Moshin inquired.

"We still suspect them of killing several Jewish civilians at the hotel bombing," Bolan replied. "And if the Samsons are responsible for that act of butchery, they sure wouldn't have any qualms about killing Arab peasants."

"If we assume Birnbaum and his friends are truly fanatics with little regard for human life—and that's too great an assumption to make at this time," Katz began, "then it's possible they carried out the attack on the village with the intention of escalating *intifadeh* violence on both sides. That would certainly suit Birnbaum's politics."

"The man is an American," Moshin reminded his two companions. "Isn't that excessive action for someone who isn't even an Israeli citizen?"

"Judging from Birnbaum's remarks, I'd say he doesn't care much about being a U.S. citizen," Bolan stated. "He considers himself to be an Israeli, and a damn militant one at that. Yakov is right. We can't assume Birnbaum and the Samson Warriors are guilty of any of the terrorist acts that have occurred since they arrived here, but they're still a very suspicious group, and stirring up trouble would fit their behavior pattern and Birnbaum's political agenda."

"Perhaps Lieutenant Yarok may learn some details as a new recruit to the Samson Warriors," Moshin said hopefully. "Director Geller wants a full report from me concerning your mission, and so far I don't have much to tell him."

"We nailed a gang of terrorists this morning," Bolan remarked. "You might remind Geller about that. Even our wrong leads have been more productive than anything the Mossad has come up with since this Samson Warrior business and the hotel bombing incident occurred."

"Unfortunately," Katz said with a sigh, "the terrorist attack on the West Bank village only supplies us with another set of questions and a new problem to deal with."

"And it may not even be connected to the hotel bombing and the alleged kidnapping of Birnbaum's friends," Bolan added. "This is like trying to put together a jigsaw puzzle with pieces that may or may not fit."

"How do we find out which pieces are the right ones?" Moshin inquired. He didn't expect either man to have an answer.

"We start by taking a closer look at each piece," the Executioner replied.

DONALD AYERS PACED the floor continuously. He was barely five feet tall and his movements and mannerisms were exaggerated as if trying to compensate for his lack of height. The guy wore an oversize suit that made him look even smaller than he actually was. His necktie was so wide that it concealed much of his white shirt. Even his watch was oversize and resembled a metal wrist weight with a clock attached.

Hal Brognola had met guys like him before. They tended to be trouble and difficult to get along with. However, there had been no way to avoid this Pentagon meet with the little guy from the State Department.

"We just received a report on the situation in Israel," Ayers announced. He had to tilt his head back to stare up at Brognola. "The *intifadeh* is worse than ever. Two major confrontations between Israelis and Arabs in the West Bank occurred within the past twenty-four hours. No idea how many people have been killed. The Mossad is sitting on the details, but my sources in Jerusalem tell me they suspect these are very serious incidents. A lot of unarmed civilians were among the victims in the last clash."

"That's why the State Department wanted to talk to me?" Brognola growled as he fished a cigar from his breast pocket. "What the hell do you expect from me, Ayers? My Ouija board is in the shop, so I can't get any secret information for you today."

"Your department was called into this matter because your people are supposed to be the best." Ayers waved his arm in an exaggerated gesture that was intended to make some sort of impression Brognola couldn't figure out. "But you don't have any information for us. Don't your superagents keep in touch with you, Brognola?"

"Not when they're in the Middle East," the big Fed replied. "Security is too tight there. There's no way to transmit a message without having a dozen intelligence outfits listening to it. The Mossad, the CIA, the NSA, the British, the French and everybody else who can tap a telephone or lock in on radio frequencies tries to get data out of the Middle East. Any Arab intel group with sophisticated communications gear tries to eavesdrop on any conversation with a hit of covert activity to it. Even some of the terrorist outfits have gotten on the high-tech bandwagon. There's no such thing as a secure line out of the Middle East."

"Then why were our State Department contacts able to contact us with information about the *intifadeh?*" Ayers asked smugly.

"What information?" Brognola countered with a shrug. "You guys don't know squat. That's why you're pestering me with this twenty questions crap. My people aren't in Israel to bring an end to the *intifadeh*. Didn't anyone tell you they were sent to find out what really happened with Birnbaum's buddies at the Tel Aviv hotel bombing?"

"And they haven't made any progress," Ayers snapped, "have they, Brognola? Things are getting worse in Israel, and your boys are spinning their goddamn wheels.''

"You got cotton in your ears, pal?" the big Fed inquired. ''I just told you they haven't been able to contact me, so I don't know what progress they've made. As for the *intifadeh*—it started years ago and didn't involve the Samson Warriors. What the hell makes you think these incidents are connected with my people's mission? Nobody said they would solve all the problems in the Middle East.''

"They've only got to solve one problem, and you admit you can't prove they're succeeding at that.'' Ayers waved both arms as if he were chasing away a swarm of horseflies. "Do you know what a tinderbox the Middle East is these days? Did you sleep through the Iraqi invasion of Kuwait? Your memory doesn't extend to when we dropped bombs on Libya or when hijacked airplanes landed in Lebanon with American citizens on board?''

"I kind of remember that stuff," Brognola said dryly, "but I can't seem to recall that the State Department did anything terribly earthshaking in response to any of it. You guys got any answers this time, or do you just feel like bitchin' at me because you figure my department is small enough that you can pass the buck to us when it comes time to pin the blame on somebody?''

"Look, Brognola—''

"No!" the big Fed said sharply. "You look, Ayers. You take a good look at me because I can have your ass bounced out of the State Department and have you reassigned as a janitor in charge of cleaning washrooms at the Capitol Building. Two of my best men are in Israel. They're putting their lives on the line because a bunch of U.S. screwballs decided to go to the Middle East to stir up trouble. None of them are worth one of my guys getting a scratch on his ass. But if those bastards got kidnapped, my men will have to rescue them."

"If they're still alive," Ayers said dryly. "You know the shit will hit the fan if any of the Samson Warriors get killed. American Jewish groups will scream their heads off and demand we increase support for Israel. Hell, Israel is already getting the biggest slice of the U.S. foreign aid pie. Imagine how thrilled U.S. taxpayers will be if we wind up sending more aid to Israel."

"To begin with," Brognola stated, "I don't think you'll get an outcry from Jewish groups here. The Jewish community finds the Samson Warriors an embarrassment and probably wishes Birnbaum and his followers would convert to Christianity. How Wonderland chooses to handle foreign aid is something I don't have any say about. My outfit has its own problems."

"Like covering up your mistakes?" Ayers asked with a sneer. "You think you can kick me out of my job, Brognola? The State Department is a hell of a lot bigger than your dirty little spy outfit or whatever you're running. Want to find out who gets the ax if we start butting heads?''

''Don't even think about playing 'you show me yours, I'll show you mine' with me, Ayers,'' the big Fed warned. ''You'll think you got porked with a telephone pole if you do.''

''Not if your people blow their mission,'' Ayers insisted, but he didn't look as confident as he tried to sound. Brognola, on the other hand, sounded as if he were serious and fully able to carry out what he claimed.

''If they do, I'll have a hell of a lot more on my mind than what you're whining about, little man.''

''I wondered when you'd stoop to insulting me because of my height!'' Ayers snapped, suddenly furious.

''That's not why you're a little man. You're petty and small-minded. You expect me to worry about the State Department getting the jitters when two of my guys might come home in body bags.''

Brognola turned on his heel and marched from the room. Ayers said something that sounded like a threat, but the man from Justice didn't even bother to glance back at the guy. He'd been concerned about Bolan and Katz already and didn't need to hear that Israel was becoming hotter by the minute.

Although Brognola hadn't admitted it to Ayers, he wondered if the reports of increased violence associated with the *intifadeh* might be connected to his men's mission. Bolan and Katz were the most experienced combat veterans among the Stony Man warriors. And that was saying something, because none of the hardcases at the Farm could be classified as cherries.

Mack Bolan had survived the jungles of Vietnam and his one-man war against the Mob. The guy's skill and resourcefulness had allowed him to triumph against incredible odds in the past. And this time he had Katz with him on the mission. The one-armed Israeli had a genius IQ, spoke six languages fluently and had a track record as impressive as Bolan's. If those two couldn't complete the mission successfully, nobody could.

Yet Brognola was a realist. He knew that no man was indestructible. The Executioner and Katz were the best at their trade, but they were still flesh and blood. They were ultratough, brilliant and their ability with weapons, strategy and survival was uncanny. Nonetheless, they were human beings, not supermen. Brognola wished they'd contact him to give a status report on the mission. He'd have been happy just to know they were still alive.

6

Lieutenant Yarok stared at the images of horror projected against the white screen. Scenes no Jew could forget appeared before the eyes of the young Israelis assembled in the bay area of the warehouse—pictures of human corpses, bones jutting from pale flesh, naked and stacked like cordwood in a communal grave. Faces of the Nazi butchers filled the screen. The soldiers seemed pleased as they examined the piles of dead collected from shower rooms that used poison gas instead of water.

Emaciated prisoners of concentration camps stood behind barbed wire. Their faces were gaunt, eyes hollow and lifeless. The Holocaust had claimed as many as six million Jews.

Yarok was moved by these scenes. Any Israeli would be. The horrors of Hitler's regime had been a lesson to Jews everywhere that they'd continue to be victims unless they became strong enough to fight back. The efforts to claim Palestine as a new Jewish homeland had started before World War II, but the Holocaust had emphasized the need for it and was directly connected with the birth of Israel.

"This is how the rest of the world treated Jews in the past," Levi Birnbaum announced from where he stood on a platform next to the screen. "The Jewish people were used as scapegoats and whipping boys in Europe for centuries before Hitler came to power. We were executed for our faith by Christian zealots during the Inquisition. We were persecuted in Russia under the czars and later by the Communists. We were corralled into ghettoes to live in poverty and despair."

Men dressed in white robes appeared on the screen. They surrounded a burning cross, the flames leaping into the dark night sky. Birnbaum introduced the Ku Klux Klan to anyone in the room not familiar with the KKK trappings.

"This is a racist organization in the United States of America," he explained. "They wear masks to hide their identity and carry out crimes against Jews and blacks in the name of 'white supremacy' and 'racial purity.' The Klan has murdered many people in the past—including Jews—yet they are allowed to have parades and rallies such as the one pictured here."

A new scene replaced the Klansmen. Men dressed in suits were assembled on a platform with swastika flags waving at each end. A beefy figure with stern features addressed an audience of short-haired males while hulking bodyguards stood beside the man's lectern.

"And here we have the American Nazi Party. This picture was taken twenty odd years ago. They call themselves by other names now, but they're still Nazis and racists. They are extremely anti-Semitic and openly display hatred toward Jews. These groups are protected by the First Amendment of the U.S. Constitution because they are granted freedom of speech."

Birnbaum clenched his fists in rage as he stared at the young Israelis. Some had been recruited into the Samson Warriors months earlier during a visit to Israel. Others were recent additions and had yet to prove themselves trustworthy enough to participate in the clandestine activities of Birnbaum's organization.

When he was sure they all shared his dream for Israel and that they were willing to do everything necessary to accomplish these goals, Birnbaum would welcome them into the heart of the Samson Warriors. He turned and pointed at the Hitler lovers on the screen.

"The United States gives people like this a right to preach hatred against Jews! And America is supposed to be Israel's greatest ally! Do any of you really believe America really cares about our country? Do we really have any allies?"

The images changed on the screen. Masked gunmen leaned from balcony rails and stared down at the Olympic Village in Munich. The crowd growled bitterly when they recognized the setting and recalled the murder of eleven Israeli athletes by Black September terrorists on September 5, 1972.

"Palestinian terrorists slaughter Jews throughout the world," Birnbaum declared. "What do the nations of the United States and Europe do in response? Nothing. Even Israel's own government has failed to react to these brutal actions with swift and deadly force.''

A bus in a ravine appeared on the screen. The Israelis recognized the incident and became even more angry. Birnbaum didn't need to explain what the scene was, but he did so, anyway.

"July 6, 1989," he began. "A Palestinian grabbed the steering wheel of Bus 405 and purposely crashed the vehicle. Sixteen people were killed. In case you don't remember, this happened here in the heart of Israel. Not far from Tel Aviv.''

The screen finally showed the burning rubble of the bomb attack at the Rishon Hotel. Birnbaum waved at the pictures and heaved his broad shoulders in an exaggerated shrug.

"Most recently Palestinian terrorists struck here. More Jews were killed and five of my fellow Warriors are still missing. What is the Israeli government doing? Where are our so-called allies? Why isn't anyone striking back at these murderers?''

He slammed a big fist into a palm and announced, "Others may play politics while our people die, but we will not! Like Samson, we are men of God and men of action. It's obvious the terrorists only understand one thing—brute force. They respect strength and power. They employ violence, and we must respond with even greater violence to stop them.''

The Israelis nodded in agreement, and someone began to cheer Birnbaum and chant his name. The others soon followed his example. Yarok joined in before he realized what he was doing, surprised to discover how effectively the Samson leader's propaganda struck home with his own emotions.

Of course, the agent believed much of what Birnbaum said was true. Jews had been victimized throughout history, and Israel was constantly threatened by its neighbors and various terrorist organizations. He'd joined the Mossad because he believed in strong national security for Israel and was prepared to fight his country's enemies wherever they might be and whoever they were. The Olympic Village murders and Bus 405 angered him and, yes, he wanted to strike back at those responsible.

Yet he also realized Birnbaum was using these incidents to exploit his own dogma. Yarok knew enough about the United States of America to appreciate the fact that the KKK and American Nazis weren't typical of U.S. citizens. The racists had freedom of speech, but so did others who disagreed with them. The latter far outnumbered the former, and America was hardly a nation that applauded anti-Semitic views.

Striking out at terrorists was fine, in Yarok's opinion, but finding the fanatic killers was easier said than done. Birnbaum was a foreigner despite his raving about being an Israeli and denouncing his native country. Who the hell was he to criticize how the Israeli government dealt with terrorism within its own borders?

If Birnbaum knew where they could locate genuine terrorist camps where murderers of Israelis were hidden, Yarok would gladly follow him and wipe out the enemy. However, Birnbaum seemed eager to label others as enemies and claim that only he and his group could save Israel. The Samson chief didn't appear to have any solutions for Israel's problems other than demands for more violence.

THE MEETING with the Israeli recruits was essentially a pep rally. Yarok and the other newcomers were told they were fine examples of Israeli manhood, true patriots and warriors who weren't afraid to fight for their country. Since Yarok was the newest man, they fussed over him more than the other recruits and told him that he'd made the right decision to become part of the Samson Warriors.

Birnbaum himself briefly spoke to the young man, embracing him and welcoming him to his first meeting. The Samson leader then crossed the bay section to a metal door, which was opened from the inside. Birnbaum entered. The door closed, and two large American-born Samson hardguys stationed themselves outside. The pair looked stern and determined to allow their boss to have some privacy.

"What's in there, Chaim?" Yarok asked one of the Israelis who had introduced himself earlier.

"That room is off-limits," the man replied. He'd been a member of the Samson Warriors longer than any of the Israeli disciples and acted as subchief among the recruits. "If you're with us long enough, you'll get to see what's in there."

"I have to earn your trust first?"

"Don't be offended," Chaim Stern urged. "We just have to take security seriously. Levi Birnbaum has many enemies. The CIA probably has his name on a hit list to be killed, and we have to be careful of the Mossad. You heard Levi criticize the government."

"The government deserves criticism," Yarok replied. "Has anyone learned any details about what happened to Mr. Birnbaum's friends?

"The men at the hotel? Not yet. They haven't made any ransom demands, and no one knows if they're alive or dead. Levi won't give in to blackmail. He doesn't believe in rewarding terrorists."

"I heard there was another gun battle between our soldiers and rebels in the West Bank."

"They aren't rebels," Stern insisted. "Those scum are PLO terrorists. They claim they're simply protesting Israeli occupation of the region, but we know they're acting on orders from Munir Kmed."

"We can never trust that man or the PLO," Yarok said with a nod. He didn't have to lie, because he believed what he told Stern. But he wasn't so sure Kmed was directly responsible for the rebels in the West Bank.

"That's very true." Stern glanced at his watch and added, "I'm afraid the meeting is over for tonight. There'll be a public rally tomorrow. We need as many present as possible so the media will see that our movement is still growing and not some passing fad."

"I'll be there," Yarok assured him.

The lieutenant and the other recruits left the warehouse. Stern supervised the inspection of the building. The Samson Warriors made certain no one was in the warehouse other than the veteran members of the organization. Birnbaum tended to distrust anyone who wasn't a Jew, but he was too quick to place total faith in anyone who was Jewish. The Samson leader was also apt to assume that any Jew who listened to his words would immediately become a convert to his cult.

Stern was more suspicious. He knew something of the cunning and machinations of the Mossad and the CIA. He'd been born and raised in Israel and known enough untrustworthy Jews to realize it was a mistake to assume too many virtues in anyone who shared his ethnic background or religion. Besides, the CIA might use an agent who could pass for an Israeli Jew, a man fluent in Hebrew and knowledgeable as a scholar in the Torah and the Talmud. Such a spy could appear to be an ideal recruit for the Samson Warriors, yet still be loyal to the interests of the American intel network.

Satisfied with his inspection, Stern knocked on the door to the "restricted" room. The metal portal opened, and Ezra Avriel's face appeared. Stern disliked the demented American and wished Birnbaum hadn't brought the man to Israel. Avriel's sleek ferret features and small cruel eyes tempted Stern to smash him in the face. The Israeli knew Avriel to be even more unpleasant than his countenance suggested.

"Did you hear what happened today?" Avriel inquired.

"I heard." Stern glanced around the room for Birnbaum, favoring to speak directly with the Samson leader rather than the unbalance Avriel.

Birnbaum sat on a bench, naked from the waist up. The big American held a dumbbell in one fist and curled his arm repeatedly. The thick biceps swelled with each repetition. Birnbaum's powerful physique was impressive, and muscles rippled across his torso as he continued the exercise.

"The building is secure, Levi," Stern announced. "Your speech was very moving. I'd say the new men are highly motivated."

"For the sake of Israel I hope you're right, Chaim. Success is with us, my friend. Ezra and his team also brought me good news."

"I thought there would be no need to launch another attack," the Israeli said with a frown. "The hotel bomb served as a cover for the men when they disappeared and pointed suspicion at the Palestinians while gaining necessary publicity for the Samson Warriors."

"And the attack on the West Bank village was also necessary," Birnbaum declared as he placed the weights on the floor. "We couldn't simply wait for the Arabs to attack an Israeli patrol first. It was necessary to provoke the confrontation."

"It was wonderful," Avriel said. "The Arabs fell like flies and the Palestinian rebel faction reacted just as we hoped. They arrived at the same time the soldiers appeared. We saw it from the road. We were already nearly a kilometer away when the terrorists and the troops began fighting."

"Some of those soldiers were killed or badly injured," Stern reminded him. "They were Israeli citizens. They were Jews protecting and serving this country."

"They were forced to do their duty against the Arab trespassers," Birnbaum replied calmly. "If Israel is to become truly strong and great, it must drive the Arabs from its land and claim more territory. The enemy will overpower us and surround Israel before gradually crushing it between them."

"I understand, Levi," Stern assured him, "but I don't like the fact that as many Israelis and Jewish tourists have been killed, since this started, as Arabs. I understood we were going to war against Munir Kmed and the PLO. Many of the Arabs killed today were civilians."

"There are no civilians," Birnbaum declared in a hard voice as he reached for his shirt. "That's the mistake we've made in the past. We've shown too much compassion toward the Arab families and so-called nonterrorists. Might I remind you that the terrorists successfully hide in Arab communities in Lebanon, the West Bank and the Gaza Strip because the 'civilians' help them.''

"The terrorists have no qualms about killing Israeli civilians," Avriel added. "Did you take a nap when the images of the Munich Massacre and Bus 405 appeared on the screen?"

"I'm painfully aware of what they've done in the past," Stern answered. "I'm just concerned that we might be regarded as terrorists by history in the future."

"Don't be silly, Chaim," Birnbaum said with a grin. "We'll be writing the history in the future. The winners of a conflict always do."

7

The moonlight reflected on the Mediterranean waters as if a giant white spotlight were beneath the surface of the sea. Mack Bolan barely glanced at the seaport as he fixed his binoculars on the warehouse along the harbor. No one was stationed outside the building, which didn't surprise the Executioner. Guards would be too obvious. The Samson Warriors certainly suspected they were under observation to some degree, and they'd try to keep as low a profile as possible while still courting the media for propaganda reasons.

"I still have some reservations about this, Mr. Pollock," Captain Moshin said softly as he sat behind the steering wheel of the Jeep. "Lieutenant Yarok's report doesn't prove the Samson Warriors are involved in anything illegal."

"Did you expect Birnbaum to tell a new recruit details about terrorist activity by his organization?" Katz asked. The one-armed commando stood by the side of the vehicle and placed an odd contraption across the hood.

The device resembled a cut-down rifle with a tele-scope attached to the frame. It was a laser micro-phone. An advanced version of a "rifle microphone," it projected a laser beam that detected sound by reg-istering vibrations on glass or metal. The beam bounced back to a receiver unit and the sounds could be heard by a headset worn by the operator.

"We don't know that the Samson Warriors are in-volved in terrorist activity," Moshin reminded the others.

"The group's a leading suspect," Bolan replied as he lowered his binoculars.

The three men were positioned near Maccabia Sta-dium, less than five hundred yards from the harbor along the coast of Tel Aviv. The laser microphone easily handled this range, and Katz locked the beam onto a barred window. He listened for sounds within the building while the Executioner attached a silencer to the threaded barrel of his Beretta 93-R and slid the pistol into a specially designed shoulder holster.

"You said this would only be reconnaissance," Moshin remarked as he stared at the holstered Ber-etta. Bolan also carried the .44 Magnum, a Ka-bar fighting knife and two wire garrotes. "Just a soft probe, you said."

"That's all I want," the big American warrior as-sured him. "But I'm going to be ready in case I get more than what I bargained for. The main item I want to check out is the room that Yarok said was off-limits to new recruits."

"Perhaps Birnbaum is staying there," Moshin suggested. "This warehouse is owned by one of his wealthier Israeli supporters. Not a member of the Samson Warriors, but a financial backer of the organization. Birnbaum and his followers are supposedly staying at a kibbutz far from the city, but he might feel more secure here."

"An observation team saw him leave hours ago," Katz reminded the captain. He still wore the headset as he spoke. "And I've only detected one set of footsteps with the laser mike. There must be a security guard or sentry inside the warehouse, but there isn't a group of men walking around inside."

"Good," Bolan replied. He was already togged in a blacksuit and had smeared his face with combat cosmetics to better blend with the night. "But I hope there's not a bunch of guys in there sitting still and not speaking to one another."

"Are you still going in?" Moshin inquired, obviously hoping the big American might change his mind.

"Yeah. Give me three minutes to get into position. You know what to do next."

"We have the easy job," Katz stated. "Be careful, Striker."

With a curt nod Bolan moved out, heading toward the building. He glided through the darkness like a wraith. Bolan was accustomed to night missions and had long ago acquired stealth that would have made an Apache brave or a Japanese ninja green with envy. Yet the Executioner didn't take anything for granted.

He never assumed his opponents would be less than fully alert and never became overconfident in his own abilities, which could lead to carelessness and, ultimately, his death.

The warrior hadn't noticed a watchman on duty at the pier, but assumed one was patrolling the harbor. Maybe more than one. He didn't want trouble with the harbor security guards. They were just doing their jobs and weren't the enemy. The Executioner would try to avoid them and enter the warehouse as discreetly as possible.

Bolan stayed alert as he advanced. He moved to a row of crates and peered between them as a flashlight beam swung across the pier.

He spotted the night watchman behind the flashlight and watched him roam the pier. The guy didn't carry a gun or nightstick. Apparently the harbor hired minimum-wage security just as most companies back in the States did. All that was required was a warm body in a uniform who was expected to watch for fire hazards and vandals because the owners discovered it was less expensive to hire guards who worked cheap than pay extra for insurance.

Bolan waited for the man to move across the pier before he left cover, approaching the warehouse from the blind side. No door or window jeopardized his surreptitious movement. However, a sturdy pipe to a rain gutter extended from the roof. The warehouse seemed ideally constructed to make Bolan's job easier.

He grabbed the drainpipe and easily climbed to the top. Hand over hand, his rubber-soled shoes pressed to the wall with each step, Bolan virtually walked up the side of the building. He hauled himself onto the roof and crept to a skylight. The Executioner reminded himself that it could all go to hell at any moment, never mind that everything had gone so smoothly thus far. Experience had taught him that danger could strike from anywhere at anytime.

The warrior looked through the glass pane of the skylight, which overlooked the bay section of the warehouse. Electric lights inside the building clearly revealed the concrete floor and wooden crates stacked along a wall. He didn't see anyone in the room below, but Katz had detected the sound of footsteps with the laser mike and someone was inside the warehouse.

Bolan examined the skylight and spotted the latch inside the window frame. There was no evidence of alarms or booby traps. Entering would be simple. From a pocket the Executioner removed a glass cutter and suction cup with a small handle, stuck the cup firmly to a pane by the latch and began to cut a circle in the glass.

A phone rang inside the warehouse. Bolan wasn't surprised and continued cutting. Captain Moshin's Mossad plant had the phone number of the warehouse. The Israeli officer had been instructed to call the number when Bolan was in position at the skylight. The ringing phone would serve as a distraction and draw the attention of the man inside the building.

The Executioner finished cutting the circle of glass and lifted it from the pane, using the suction cup and handle. Then he reached inside, unfastened the latch, opened the window and slipped through the skylight.

The phone stopped ringing as he gripped the sill and hung full-length, arms completely extended. A voice spoke within the bay area, and Bolan heard the telephone receiver click as it was returned to the cradle. He glanced around, but didn't see anyone, so he released his hold on the windowsill and dropped to the floor, landing silently as he bent his knees to absorb the impact.

The Executioner headed for the crates and knelt beside them in the shadows. He waited for the unseen man to appear, which didn't take long. The guy emerged from a tiny office, muttering something in Hebrew. Bolan saw the guy clearly from his hiding place. He was young and well built and moved in the coordinated manner of a fighter with well-trained reflexes. A pistol was holstered on the man's hip, but he didn't carry a weapon in his hands.

The Executioner silently crept up behind the man. He had no wish to harm him and planned to seize the guard from behind, kick the back of a knee to bring the man down and render him unconscious with a blow behind the ear. Bolan raised his hands and prepared to lunge.

The man turned suddenly, sensing danger, and slashed a cross-body karate chop at Bolan, reacting to the immediate threat with instincts conditioned by training in self-defense.

The Executioner grabbed the man's arm near the wrist and elbow to stop the attack before the guy could land a blow. He moved with the flow of the striking limb and used the attacker's momentum to his advantage. Bolan turned, pulled with one hand and pushed with the other. The guard's arm locked at the elbow, and pressure at the shoulder brought him to his toes.

The guy hurled forward, forced to go with the motion of his captured limb or suffer a broken arm. He whirled head over heels and crashed to the hard floor. Bolan held on to the guy's wrist and attempted a blow to the nerve center at the armpit below the extended limb. The fallen sentry rolled back on his shoulders and kicked up from the floor. His boot hit Bolan in the chest and staggered him.

The Israeli broke free and scrambled to his feet, reaching for the gun on his hip. Bolan almost drew his Beretta from shoulder leather, but hesitated. He didn't want to kill a man who might simply be protecting property and not connected with any sort of terrorist activity. However, the guard showed no concern for Bolan's well-being and yanked his pistol from its holster.

Bolan grabbed the guy's gun with his right hand and shoved it toward the floor. His left fist smashed into the guard's jaw. The sentry's head recoiled from the punch as Bolan snap-kicked the man in the abdomen. He gripped the wrist above the gun with both hands and wrenched forcibly. Fingers opened and the pistol fell to the floor. Bolan swept a boot to the weapon and kicked it across the room and beyond his opponent's reach.

The guard reached for the warrior's face, fingers arched into claws aimed at the Executioner's eyes. Bolan jerked his head back to avoid the slashing fingernails and pulled the captive wrist to keep his opponent off balance. Then, suddenly, he released the guy and stepped forward, his arm raised high. Bending his elbow, he slammed it into the side of his adversary's head. The blow drove the guard to his knees. Stunned and on all fours, the man was no longer a threat. Bolan picked his next shot and knocked the guy unconscious with the final blow.

The soft probe hadn't gone as smoothly as Bolan had hoped, but he hadn't been forced to kill the guard. The man would be unconscious for a few minutes, and the warrior would use that time to check the mysterious "restricted room." Whether he would question the sentry or leave before the guy awoke would depend on what he found in the room. He turned to face the metal door and reached into a pocket for a set of lockpicks. But the door burst open and armed hardguys charged from the room.

The Executioner's battle-honed reflexes commanded his body. He reacted instantly to the unexpected threat and hurled himself to the floor, drawing his Beretta before he hit the concrete and slid for the cover of the platform. An automatic weapon roared, the muzzle-flash burning from an Uzi submachine gun in the fists of his closest adversary. The guy had opened fire a split second too late, and the bullets ripped air above Bolan's prone body.

The warrior triggered the 93-R on semiauto mode. The double-action pistol barked twice, the report muffled by the silencer. Both Parabellum rounds tore into the upper torso of the SMG-wielding hardguy, who toppled backward as he fired his weapon. An arch of 9 mm hornets slashed into the ceiling and shattered the skylight. The man's weapon ceased fire and glass showered down on his corpse.

Bolan slid along the base of the platform as other gunners sprayed the bay area with a hailstorm of high-velocity slugs. Bullets splintered wood from the platform and nearby crates. The warrior stayed low and crawled to the corner of the platform. He thumbed the fire selector to 3-round burst and thrust the Beretta over the top. The enemy fire ceased as the gunmen were unsure where their opponent was located. Bolan found two of his adversaries at the opposite end of the platform. They were clad only in undershorts, but carried Galil rifles and ammo belts with magazine pouches slung across their shoulders.

The men had apparently been asleep in the room and had been roused by the sounds of Bolan's fight with the guard. He wasn't certain how many hard-guys had emerged from the room, but they were well armed and intended to deal with the intruder with deadly force.

However, Mack Bolan was an expert on the subject. He fired the 93-R and drilled one man with a trio of 9 mm destroyers. The silenced Beretta coughed harshly, and the Executioner shifted his aim to the second gunman. The guy's ears were ringing from the effects of full-auto firearms unleashed in a confined area. He didn't hear the muted report of Bolan's weapon or notice the muzzle-flash, because the silencer reduced the glare of the Beretta barrel, as well. The guy's comrade began to fall, his head split open by Bolan's first volley.

Too late, the second gunner realized what had happened and tried to swing his assault rifle toward Bolan's position. The Executioner nailed him with another 3-round burst of Beretta slugs. The guy's nose vanished as bullets knifed through his face and chopped into his brain. He collapsed to the floor as more enemy fire forced Bolan to duck behind his cover.

The full-auto salvo chipped wood from the edge of the platform, and tiny pieces pelted the Executioner as he hugged the floor. His opponents had him pinned down with inadequate cover, and he couldn't crawl to the crates without presenting a clear target. They could easily keep him trapped and position themselves for a cross-fire attack. Bolan had to act quickly or he'd leave the warehouse in a body bag.

The Executioner drew the Desert Eagle and shoved the Beretta across the floor toward the crates. The 93-R slid into clear view of the enemy. The barrage of full-auto fire ceased abruptly when the gunmen saw the Beretta. They wondered if the mysterious intruder was dead or wounded. It seemed unlikely he would discard the fearsome 9 mm pistol by choice....

Bolan hoped his gamble worked as he swung the Eagle over the platform corner. A startled figure stared into the muzzle of the big Magnum pistol. He would have been a ridiculous figure, dressed in his skivvies with his mouth open and eyes bulging with surprise, but the Galil rifle in his hands was not amusing. Bolan fired the pistol and hit the guy with a mighty .44 Magnum round to the left of the breastbone. The force of the bullet blew the man off his feet and dumped him onto the floor, out of the battle forever.

Another gun-toting figure swung his Uzi at Bolan and bolted for cover by a row of crates, firing on the run. The 9 mm rounds plowed into the platform near the Executioner, but the gunner's aim was too hasty to be accurate. Bolan ducked nonetheless. He also noticed no one else had opened fire on his position. The guy with the Uzi was the last underwear-clad opponent.

A big sliding door to the bay section tore loose from its track and fell inward at a crooked angle. A headlight and the grille at the nose of a Jeep appeared in the gap. Moshin sat at the wheel of the vehicle, which was equipped with a steel pipe battering ram under the front fender. The Mossad officer had used it effectively to hammer down the door.

The gunman whirled to face the unexpected attack. Katz already had the guy in his sights. The one-armed Phoenix commander knelt in the back of the Jeep and triggered his own Uzi before the enemy could fire an SMG. A trio of Parabellum rounds ripped through the gunner's chest and sent him hurtling backward into the crates. His body slumped to the concrete, vital organs terminated by the 9 mm missiles.

Movement drew Bolan's attention, and he turned to see that the guard had regained consciousness quicker than he had anticipated.

The tough guy had also gathered up a Galil from one of the slain gunmen. He pointed the assault rifle at the Jeep in the doorway. Bolan snap-aimed his Desert Eagle, relying on instinct and skill developed by years of training and combat. The big .44 bellowed, and the familiar recoil rode his arm from wrist to shoulder.

A 200-grain hollowpoint struck the enemy gunman under the left shoulder blade. It burrowed through his heart, obliterating the organ, and blasted an exit wound in the guard's chest as big as a pocket watch. The Galil slipped from trembling fingers as the man performed a convulsive dance of death and collapsed on the floor.

"Mr. Pollock?" Captain Moshin called out as he opened the door to the Jeep.

"I'm all right," Bolan assured him as he retrieved his Beretta 93-R. "The night watchman will probably call the local police. You'd better be ready to talk to them, Captain."

Moshin nodded. He'd drawn his pistol, a .357 Magnum Desert Eagle, and entered the warehouse. Katz was already inside. The one-armed commando carried his Uzi canted on a shoulder and pointed at the ceiling. He was confident that all the enemy had been taken out of action because Bolan stood clearly in the open instead of remaining near cover.

"Did you manage to take any of them alive?" Katz inquired.

"Almost," Bolan answered, and tilted his head at the slain guard. "This guy was too tough for his own good. He should have stayed down while he still had a pulse, but he forced me to put him down for keeps."

"These other fellows appear to have gone to battle in a hurry," Katz commented when he noticed that the remaining five corpses were dressed only in their underwear. "I didn't hear any of them when I used the laser mike. Apparently none of them snored."

"They were in the room Yarok said was off-limits," Bolan explained. "No windows on that side of the building. The laser only picked up sound within this section."

"I don't imagine they were staying here because they couldn't afford hotel rooms," Katz said as he walked to one of the dead men.

"Why were they hiding in that room?" Moshin asked. He didn't expect Bolan or Katz to be able to answer him.

But Katz surprised him. "I've seen this man's face before." He looked down at the dead foe and added, "We all did. He was one of the five American Samson Warriors who allegedly disappeared during the bomb attack at the hotel."

Moshin said something in Hebrew, his tone and expression filled with amazement. Bolan was surprised, as well. He looked at another corpse and recognized the dead man's face. A photograph of him had been in a file concerning one of Birnbaum's missing comrades.

"Here's another one," he announced. "All five of our sleeping beauties are probably the guys Birnbaum claimed had been abducted by Palestinian terrorists. They've been hiding here at the warehouse in the restricted room."

"What on earth is Birnbaum planning?" Moshin wondered aloud.

"Whatever it is," Bolan replied, "I doubt it has much to do with peace on earth or goodwill toward men."

8

They found six bunks. The beds were stacked double-decker style as used in military barracks. Five beds were in disarray, sheets rumbled and hastily pushed aside. The sixth bed was still neatly made with the sheets tucked under the mattress with "hospital corners." However, only five duffel bags were by the bunks.

"Easy to tell which beds the Samsons were sleeping in," Moshin remarked. "Do you suppose the sixth bunk belonged to the man on guard duty?"

"Maybe," Bolan answered with a shrug. He noticed a picture of Munir Kmed nailed to a wall with three darts stuck in the PLO leader's face. "Let's check their gear."

The duffel bags were opened and the contents dumped onto the floor. Among the clothes were Israeli army uniform shirts and trousers, gas masks and boots. Bolan inspected a shirt from one of the bags. His expression grew grim, his eyes as hard as diamonds and his mouth set in a firm line. Katz used the hooks of his prosthesis to pick up a gas mask by a strap.

"Looks like we found the scum responsible for the slaughter of the Arabs in the West Bank, as well," Katz announced, and tossed the mask onto the floor.

"Are you sure?" Moshin asked with surprise. "I know the killers wore gas masks, but that isn't adequate proof the Samson Warriors were involved."

"These army fatigues don't have unit crests or ranks," Bolan declared, discarding the shirt. "That also fits the identity of the assassins we saw on the videotape. Six killers and six bunks."

"The lack of unit crest doesn't prove anything, either," Moshin insisted. "I would rather believe the men responsible for the carnage in the West Bank were Birnbaum's people instead of Israeli soldiers."

"Have the ballistics checked on the weapons used by these bastards," Katz instructed Moshin. "If the bullets match with the slugs found in the murdered Arab villagers, we'll have all the proof we need."

"We have it already," the Executioner said in a hard voice. "Maybe there isn't enough evidence to satisfy a court, but we know Birnbaum is responsible. We know he set off the bomb at the Rishon Hotel and killed several innocent people just to cover the disappearance of these men supposedly kidnapped by the PLO."

"And he used the incident for propaganda and publicity," Katz added.

"We also know the five missing Samsons were staying here," Bolan said. "They were hidden from investigators or the press and carried out the hit on the Arab village, deliberately planned to trigger a fire-fight between Israeli soldiers and Arab rebels. We know Birnbaum will continue these acts of violence unless we stop him. That's all we need to know to justify going after our next target."

"Birnbaum," Moshin agreed with a nod. "He and the rest of the Samson Warriors have been staying at a kibbutz populated by sympathizers of his organization. I can assemble a company of paratroopers to participate in a raid in a matter of hours."

Sirens wailed outside the warehouse. The sounds drew closer, and Bolan reminded Moshin that he would have to use his Mossad status to deal with the local authorities. The captain headed for the entrance of the building to meet the police while the Executioner and Katz hastily searched the rest of the warehouse.

The crates appeared to be legitimate import-export merchandise, but there wasn't time to inspect every case. The Mossad and the cops would have to handle that task. The Stony Man pair checked the tiny office, which was smaller than most closets. There was barely enough room for a desk and two chairs, but a shortwave radio was located on a shelf in addition to a telephone.

"Looks like a miniature communications center," Bolan remarked. "Birnbaum must have remained in contact with the men here fairly often. They might have used some sort of spot checks with radio signals sent every hour to let the base know everything was okay at the warehouse.''

''The shortwave wouldn't be any more secure than the telephone,'' Katz added with a nod. ''Not in Israel. Birnbaum would know this and some of the Israelis associated with him would surely tell him if he didn't. They probably use something like Morse code to send signals with the radio. No point trying to guess what the code might be. It could be a word, a series of numbers or simply a short dot or a long dash.''

''And we have no idea how long ago the last signals were exchanged. If Birnbaum's people try to contact this site, or fail to get the signal if the guy here is supposed to send it, they'll suspect something happened. Terrorists are notoriously paranoid. They might bolt from the kibbutz if they think this place has been burned.''

''Maybe not immediately,'' Katz said. ''The Samson commo people might wait a few minutes or even longer if the signal isn't received on time. They might transmit a signal repeatedly for several minutes before they decide there won't be a response. How soon they can strike camp and run depends on how well prepared Birnbaum's forces are for such an emergency. Perhaps they're overconfident.''

''We can't count on that,'' Bolan replied. ''It's also possible they won't run, or they'll prepare to fight while getting ready to bug out of the kibbutz.''

"We could be wrong," Katz said hopefully. "The radio might simply be here because Birnbaum is worried about having the phone tapped, or as a method of eavesdropping on radio messages in the area. They might not have set up any system of codes and signals."

"We'd better expect the worst," the Executioner insisted. "Let's tell Moshin to hurry up with the police because we have to get to that kibbutz as fast as possible. I hope he can get those paratroopers ready double-quick. We might have one hell of a fight on our hands before this is over."

CAPTAIN MOSHIN DIDN'T disappoint Bolan. The Mossad officer contacted his director, and an hour later a company of crack troops from the Independent Paratroop Battalion met Bolan, Katz and Moshin outside Tel Aviv. The soldiers were ready for action, and packed Galil rifles, grenades and fighting knives. The troops also had three NATO FALO machine guns and several MK-19 grenade launchers.

The company commander was a senior captain. He understood that the Mossad agent and the two foreigners were in charge and didn't complain. Transportation consisted of three trucks large enough to carry the men and equipment. A fully armed gunship could also be contacted by radio for air support.

Katz and Moshin briefed the officers in Hebrew to make certain there would be no misunderstanding about the target. The soldiers were surprised to learn a kibbutz was the chosen site for a raid on terrorists and even more surprised to discover Levi Birnbaum's Samson Warriors were the enemy. However, they had orders from battalion command and had been told that the emergency mission had been authorized by the Mossad.

The strategy was based on limited information about the kibbutz. They knew the location of the farming community and its size, but they could only guess how many people might live there or what sort of weapons their opponents might have. Since a kibbutz was a type of communal farm, families were located at the site. This meant they had to expect women, children and other noncombatants. The raiders would have to try to protect the innocent bystanders while dealing with the terrorists. It was unlikely that the Samson Warriors would give up without a fight, and previous actions revealed Birnbaum and his followers had little concern for the lives of innocent people.

The trucks headed north, separating as they approached the kibbutz and driving onto dirt roads to advance on the farm from different directions. Bolan and Moshin rode in one truck to command the men within. Katz was in charge of another section of the assault force, and the company commander had the third vehicle and remaining troops. They remained in radio contact.

They converged on the kibbutz. Men emerged from the trucks and headed for the community on foot. The commune was small, consisting of less than a square mile of land with tomato crops, a few citrus trees and a flock of sheep. The houses were small and designed in a practical manner to endure harsh weather.

"Tell the men to stay alert," the Executioner instructed Captain Moshin, "but not to jump to conclusions if they see movement by a window or door. Take cover at the slightest hint of a threat, but don't open fire unless it's necessary."

"We're all concerned about the innocents," Moshin assured him.

"There might not be any terrorists here. Birnbaum and his group must have transportation. Probably more than those two pickups parked over there. The enemy might have already bolted. Pass the word to the men not to get trigger-happy. That goes double for the guys with grenade launchers. I don't want anyone blowing up a house because some kid pulls back a curtain to look outside."

Despite the warning, Bolan stayed low and held his M-16 at the ready in case he was wrong. He was confident Katz had also noticed the lack of vehicles at the kibbutz and given similar instructions to the men under his command. The assault unit had to take extra care to avoid harming innocents, yet remain prepared for danger.

The raiders surrounded the kibbutz and gradually made their way through the fields of tomatoes and diminutive orchards. They watched for booby traps and mines, but encountered neither device. A voice bellowed from a bullhorn in Hebrew to announce that the farm was surrounded by heavily armed soldiers acting on the authority of the Israeli government. The people inside the houses were ordered to come out with their hands raised and were warned that any resistance would force the troops to respond accordingly.

Doors opened and several women and children stepped from the farmhouses. Several soldiers moved forward, covered by other troops, and ordered the civilians to walk away from their dwellings. Bolan headed for the nearest building, followed by two paratroopers. He glimpsed movement throughout the kibbutz, but only saw uniformed members of the assault team rushing into position either to investigate structures or supply backup.

The Executioner entered the house, M-16 braced at his hip. He scanned the room within, rifle barrel moving with his eyes. The place was deserted except for a gray-haired figure seated in front of a low table. Bolan pointed his weapon at the man as the wheelchair rolled away from the table. The chair turned, and the owner stared at Bolan's rifle with anger rather than fear. Both of his legs had been amputated at the knee.

"Keep your hands where I can see them," Bolan warned.

"You want to finish the job the Palestinians started ten years ago?" the older man asked in fluent English. "Are you afraid of a cripple in a wheelchair?"

"That doesn't mean you're helpless. Just keep your hands at shoulder level." The warrior spotted a shortwave radio on the table.

The Israeli smiled and placed his hands on his head, interlacing the fingers. "You're too late," he announced smugly. "They're gone."

"You spoke with Birnbaum on that?" the Executioner inquired as he pointed at the radio with his rifle.

"I told him not to come back," the man confirmed. "I don't know where they've gone, and I wouldn't tell you if I did. My only regret is that I'm not whole and couldn't go with them."

"Those women and kids outside have a few more reasons for regrets," Bolan commented.

"Their husbands and fathers are part of a brave movement that will make Israel so powerful no one will ever dare attack another Jew again," the man stated. "You can't stop them. No one can."

"Yeah? We'll see about that."

9

The young Israelis were confused and concerned as the morning sun grew steadily hotter. They frequently checked their watches and expressed opinions and theories about Levi Birnbaum. The rally should have begun more than an hour ago, but there was no sign of the American firebrand or the veteran members of the Samson Warriors.

Lieutenant Yarok could have told them. The young Mossad officer had been informed about the events at the warehouse and the disappointing raid on the kibbutz. He would have been astonished if Birnbaum or any of his top Samson cronies had shown their faces at the public rally. The event was held near the diamond exchange in Tel Aviv. The rally site was also close to the north station for the city bus service. It was a good choice to attract crowds and media attention, but Birnbaum would have to be a fool to appear at the demonstration.

However, the Mossad still wanted Yarok to attend because there was a slim chance Chaim Stern or one of the other Israeli Samson subchiefs might arrive and contact the recruits who had attended the private meeting at the warehouse the night before. Yarok considered this to be a waste of time. In Yarok's opinion none of Birnbaum's inner circle of Samson Warriors would risk capture to get in touch with new recruits whom they still didn't fully trust.

Of course, Yarok was a junior officer and not in a position to argue with his superiors. He stood among the group of Samson supporters and pretended to be as worried about Birnbaum's welfare as the others. He glanced at the policemen who ringed the crowd for potential riot control. He thought this was one occasion the Tel Aviv law-enforcement officers didn't need to bother observing the rally. Without Birnbaum to stir up the crowd with fiery speeches, the would-be Samson members would eventually give up and go home.

Yarok was tempted to leave, but decided it would be better if he waited for some of the others to abandon the vigil first. He didn't want to be remembered as the newest recruit who got bored and left before the rest of the group realized the rally was a no-show. There was still a chance that someone connected with Birnbaum's elite Samsons might try to contact recruits in the days to come. However, it seemed obvious the American fanatic wasn't going to attend or send a representative. Yarok raised his wrist to consult his watch, wondering how much longer he'd have to wait for someone else to decide this exercise in ennui wasn't worth continuing.

A young zealot in the crowd began shouting that something sinister must have happened to Birnbaum. Another voice expressed concern that their leader might have been kidnapped or killed by the PLO, but someone else assured him that one of the other Samsons would have come to the rally to report this terrible news.

The youth who first voiced his opinion about Birnbaum's fate announced his suspicion that the Israeli government and the American CIA had probably conspired to censor the Samson Warriors. Birnbaum and his closest followers were probably being detained by the authorities because the "spineless traitors in Jerusalem" wanted to silence the Samson movement. He turned to face Yarok and asked if he agreed.

The Mossad lieutenant prepared to reply in the manner fitting his false identity. Suddenly the other man's head snapped back violently. Blood and brain matter burst from his shattered skull as the report of a rifle cracked above the sounds of the chattering crowd. Yarok jumped away from the fatally wounded youth. The guy's eyes bulged and his tongue hung from his open mouth as he sank to the pavement. The astonished and silly expression was frozen on his lifeless face.

The crowd reacted with cries of alarm, scattering in all directions. Yarok tried to run for cover, but two Samson sympathizers collided with him and blocked the Mossad man's path. Terrible pain filled Yarok's chest when hot projectiles smashed flesh and bone. His legs seemed unable to support him, and he dropped to the pavement. The screams and shouts of the crowd were muffled as the agent's hearing rapidly faded. More shots were fired, but the sound seemed to come from the end of a tunnel. The pain was replaced by numbness.

The Mossad agent was vaguely aware that he was dying. It didn't frighten him as much as he would have expected had he known that day would be his last. He wondered what would happen to his family and how his parents would handle the news of his death. His last thought was a memory from his childhood of being held close in his mother's arms.

THE CROWD SCATTERED as a burst of automatic fire raked the streets. Lieutenant Yarok and two other victims already lay dead on the pavement. Others fell, wounded by the steady streams of bullets.

The Tel Aviv police saw the lone gunman on a hotel rooftop. The figure aimed an AK-47 assault rifle at the crowd and fired without apparent concern for who might be among the victims. A keffiyeh concealed the gunman's features. The police hadn't expected trouble in the form of a sniper. They'd prepared for riots or conflicts between Samson supporters and counter-demonstrators. They hadn't anticipated such an attack on the rally.

A police lieutenant rapidly ordered patrolmen to herd the crowd to cover while others cut off the street at both ends to keep civilians out of the danger zone and formed barricades to prevent the assassin—or assassins—from fleeing the area. A dozen policemen were sent to the hotel, weapons primed to take on the gunman.

Two cops covered the front of the building and another pair moved to the rear. The rest entered the lobby. A police sergeant stopped at the front desk while armed men rushed to the elevators and stairwells. Hotel guests stood clear of the gun-toting officers, confused and frightened by the violence.

"We need to cover every exit from the roof," the sergeant told the desk clerk. "Is there any other way from the roof other than the elevator or the stairs?"

"How do I know?" the clerk replied with exasperation. "I just work here. I didn't design the hotel."

"Never mind. We'll find out when we get up there. Did you see an Arab come into the hotel?"

"An Arab?"

Elevator doors rolled open, and two policemen pointed pistols at the man inside the car. He stared at them in surprise, round-eyed, and held his hands at shoulder level. The guy appeared harmless, dressed in a short-sleeve white shirt and slacks, with no visible weapons.

"What the hell's going on?" he demanded in English, his accent labeling him as American. "The shooting is upstairs. Why hassle me?"

"Please come here, sir," the sergeant urged. "I need to speak with you."

"Okay," the American answered, stepping from the elevator.

The two officers entered the car and punched the button to the top story. The police sergeant asked to see the American's passport. The guy nodded and handed it over.

"Ezra Avriel?" the sergeant inquired.

"That's what it says," the American replied with a sigh. "Look, I was just visiting a friend of mine who's staying at this hotel. I've got an appointment to keep with a tour group."

"You ought to remain inside until we've taken care of the gunman on the roof. It isn't safe outside."

"Not safe inside if you ask me," Avriel snorted. "I heard the shots, for crying out loud. You guys have the bastard trapped in here. I don't care to hang around. Sorry if that sounds chickenshit, but I'm just a tailor from Chicago."

"A sniper fired on the crowd outside," the sergeant insisted as he returned the passport. "We can't protect you if you leave the building."

"The shooting stopped. He's probably not on the roof anymore, and you know it. I heard about that bomb attack at the Rishon Hotel. How do you know this lunatic won't do the same thing here?"

"We don't know if there's one sniper or a number of men involved," the sergeant replied. "We don't know if the shooting has really stopped or may continue when the gunman or gunmen move into a new position."

"Are you going to arrest me?" Avriel demanded. "Am I being held against my will? Maybe I should call the U.S. embassy."

"That's not necessary," the officer assured Avriel. He had already wasted too much time with the tourist and needed to concentrate on locating the sniper. "You understand the risks involved. If you insist on leaving, I won't detain you."

"Thank you, Officer." Avriel headed for the door.

He passed the cops outside the building without being stopped or questioned. He wasn't dressed in Arab garb or carrying an AK-47. There was no reason to suspect him, and the police assumed he had been cleared and allowed to leave the hotel. Avriel suppressed a smile as he walked from the building. He'd been confident he could bluff his way out of the hotel, and he was equally sure he'd be able to escape from the scene before anyone learned his presence in the area was more than happenstance.

Avriel stayed clear of the rally site. Despite his confidence and arrogance that he could waltz past the police, the man was worried about getting close enough to the would-be recruits to be recognized. Birnbaum had kept Avriel away from the previous Samson rallies in Tel Aviv, but the Samson fanatic still feared he might be noticed by the surviving young zealots.

The Samson killer moved to the police blockade at the end of the street. He had to show his passport again, and the American ID satisfied the cops. After all, the man they wanted had been wearing Arab clothing complete with keffiyeh. Avriel was permitted to move on and soon approached the bus station.

He waited for a bus to take him to Hayarkon Park where he'd left his Toyota rental. Ezra Avriel was pleased. He thought it had been a good day's work.

10

Captain Moshin slammed the telephone receiver into the cradle, then stared across his desk at Mack Bolan. The Executioner had learned of Lieutenant Yarok's death and the sniper attack on the Samson supporters in Tel Aviv. He guessed Moshin had received more information about the incident, which had been less than encouraging news.

"Avriel was there," the captain announced bitterly. "The bastard showed the police his passport. He didn't even bother to use a forgery."

"Maybe he didn't have one. I remember Avriel's name from the files because the man is a certified mental case. He might be demented enough to think it doesn't matter if people know he was at the shooting site. He might even want them to know for some twisted reason. Might figure he'll be acknowledged as a hero when some fantasy victory unfolds for the Samson Warriors."

"What's disgusting is he walked right through the police surrounding the hotel and covering the street exits," Moshin declared. "The police were looking for an Arab gunman. It didn't occur to them that the keffiyeh might have been a disguise. Even when they found the discarded headgear, robe and Kalashnikov rifle on the hotel roof, the police still wasted time interrogating Arab employees."

"And no one knows what happened to Avriel," Bolan said with a sigh. "He got away. We know that much."

"Not very helpful."

"It wasn't a very positive event," the Executioner replied. "Avriel almost certainly acted on his own. I think Birnbaum is too careful and intelligent to order the attack on his supporters at the rally. It was too risky and unnecessary. Birnbaum is smart enough to keep a low profile after the raid on the warehouse last night."

"Why did Avriel open fire on the rally?" Moshin wondered aloud. "Was it just to stir more propaganda against Arabs in Israel and cause more sympathy for the Samson Warriors?"

"It could be Avriel guessed Yarok was a spy. The lieutenant was the most recent recruit, and the raid followed his visit at the Samson meeting in the warehouse. Avriel might have killed him for revenge."

"But he couldn't have known Yarok was a Mossad agent," Moshin declared. "And he killed two others and wounded five more supporters of the Samson Warriors."

"You think he cares?" Bolan replied. "None of the Samson Warriors seem to have much regard for human life. Avriel is crazy, so he's probably even less concerned about killing innocent bystanders than the other terrorists. If Yarok wasn't a spy, Avriel could still justify the attack because it made martyrs of Samson supporters. Since Birnbaum and his inner circle of friends have to stay in hiding, they can't add the recruits to their ranks now, anyway. Looking at it from that point of view, with no restrictions caused by morality, the potential recruits were more valuable as dead martyrs for the cause.''

"And Avriel was disguised as an Arab, so the shooting will escalate hostilities between Jews and Arabs," Moshin said grimly. "Unfortunately the news report of the sniper attack will say the gunman was an Arab."

"When is the government going to tell the press about Birnbaum and the Samson Warriors? We already found the five 'kidnapped' members at the warehouse."

"But ballistics still haven't proved the weapons used by those men were the murder weapons employed by the masked attackers in the West Bank. Even if we can confirm this, it doesn't prove Birnbaum ordered the attack. Critics might claim the Israeli military is using the ballistics reports to match weapons used by its own and saying that the guns were found with the slain Samson Warriors. Scapegoats."

"So we have to find Birnbaum and the others," Bolan said as he checked his watch. "Where's Katz? I thought he finished questioning the people from the kibbutz."

"He did," Moshin answered. "Director Geller wanted to talk to him concerning the mission. The colonel didn't see any reason you should meet with the director and said you wouldn't want to do so, anyway."

"He's right. As long as we're here, let's make the most of the Mossad's data-gathering network—establish computer links with police throughout the country, see about getting cooperation from the CIA and NSA to tap into their sources of information, as well. Hopefully one of these links will give us a lead to the Samson Warriors' location."

"Very well," Captain Moshin agreed. "I hope this works. Birnbaum's group might go underground so deep that it could take months to find them."

"They won't stay inactive that long," the Executioner corrected. "The Samson Warriors came to Israel to carry out a definite agenda. They aren't finished yet, and whatever they plan to do they won't stop now."

DIRECTOR GELLER glanced down at the typed report form on his desk. The Mossad boss frowned and raised his eyes to stare at Yakov Katzenelenbogen. Geller's expression suggested he was unhappy with the report. Katz had expected this, but wasn't disturbed by the director's opinion. He no longer worked for the Mossad. Pleasing Geller wasn't necessary.

"This report lacks details, Colonel," Geller declared, stabbing an index finger at the papers. "We need more information."

"Captain Moshin will present a full report when the mission is complete," Katz answered as he took a seat in a chair facing the director's desk. "We're currently too busy to waste time with paperwork."

"You always were difficult, Colonel," the director complained.

Katz didn't respond. Geller referred to him as "colonel" because that was Katz's former rank while an officer in the Mossad. The director recalled Katz's career with Israeli intelligence well enough to know the man wasn't always a strict team player and occasionally handled operations with little regard for politics. But he was also highly successful in the field.

"This report suggests Birnbaum and the Samson Warriors are responsible for violence in the West Bank and other incidents that appear to be Arab terrorism," Geller commented. "The proof of these claims seems less than convincing."

"What we know and what we can prove are two different matters," Katz explained as he removed a pack of cigarettes from a pocket. "But we're sure the Samson Warriors are responsible for everything mentioned in the report."

"You and 'Mr. Pollock' seem positive these acts of terrorism were carried out by Jews," Geller said dryly. "American Jews working with Israelis."

"Don't tell me you're going to accuse me of being anti-Semitic," Katz remarked with a slight smile.

"Hardly," the director replied gruffly. "I know you, Colonel. You don't have much concern for public relations or the Mossad's image. You also don't appear terribly concerned about relations between the United States and Israel. Indeed, Israel's relations with the entire nation could be in jeopardy."

"Because we discovered a handful of Jewish terrorists?" Katz asked with a raised eyebrow. "The Samson Warriors are fanatics."

"You know that and I know that," Geller confirmed, "but our enemies will use this information to fuel flames of prejudice against Israel and Jews living in every country on earth. I don't need to remind you that we live under a constant threat of Arab aggression. The last mission you and the four men you usually work with conducted in Israel was against an Arab terrorist outfit modeled in the manner of the ancient order of Assassins."

"They were fanatics, too," Katz reminded Geller. "The Assassins were Muslin extremists and were no more typical of Islam than the Samson Warriors are of Judaism."

"Really? You seem to forget international state-sponsored terrorism conducted by the governments of Iran, Libya, Syria and Iraq in the past two decades. That doesn't include the Palestinian terrorist groups or the military aggressions carried out by Saddam Hussein."

"And you use these incidents to condemn Islam?" Katz inquired, shaking his head. "You know better than that. Iraq invaded Kuwait and Hussein threatened Saudi Arabia as well as Israel and America. The conference of Arab leaders held in Egypt following the invasion condemned Hussein's actions. The vast majority of Arab nations opposed Iraq's behavior. To Arabs, Israeli occupation of the West Bank and Gaza Strip are unacceptable. If you and I were Arabs, we would probably feel the same way."

"An odd remark for a man I've always regarded as a good Jew and a defender of both the State of Israel and the United States of America," Geller commented.

"As a good Jew, I look to the Talmud, which teaches that a wise man learns from everyone," Katz stated. "That means one learns from the Arabs and Muslims, as well. You can't learn from someone if you refuse to listen to them or see things from their point of view. The Talmud also states that an honored person is one who honors others and a truly strong person is one who controls his impulses. Prejudice is impulsive and honors neither the bigot nor the one he is bigoted against."

Geller didn't reply. He regretted his previous remarks and wished he hadn't tried to appeal to Katzenelenbogen on an emotional level. The one-armed commando was a scholar and favored reason and logic in an argument. The man was also familiar with the scriptures. This left the director little ammunition to use in the debate.

"As for my patriotism toward either the United States or Israel," Katz continued, "I'll let my record in service to both countries speak on that."

"I didn't question your patriotism," Geller said quickly. "I have great admiration and respect for you, Colonel. Yet, you fail to understand how the Samson Warriors' terrorism can cause problems for Israel. The United States is bound to criticize us for killing American Jews even if they are terrorists. After all, their terrorism is ultimately directed against Arab states in a twisted effort to make Israel stronger."

"That's exactly why the United States and other countries will applaud Israel for refusing to accept Jewish terrorism as surely as it condemns terrorism by Muslim or Christian fanatics," Katz insisted. "The Samson Warriors must be stopped because what they're doing is wrong. They're also killing Israeli citizens as well as Arabs. It happened again this morning. One of your own men was among the victims."

"I know about Lieutenant Yarok's murder," Geller said grimly, "but the gunman was described as an Arab."

"He was dressed as an Arab," Katz corrected. "That's not the same thing. We need time to prove what the Samson Warriors really are. We need the Mossad's cooperation, as well."

"You had Israeli soldiers raid a kibbutz and arrest Israeli citizens whom we can't prove committed any crime," Geller said with a sigh. "You tell me they collaborated with Birnbaum's people to accomplish some sort of conspiracy that still doesn't seem clear. What do these people hope to accomplish, Colonel?"

"We're still working on learning that information."

"You'd better have some success soon," the director warned. "If you and your comrade-in-arms haven't produced more positive results within the next forty-eight hours, I'll be forced to expel you both from Israel as undesirables."

11

Jerusalem has been called the holiest city in the world. Many would agree with this claim. The Executioner had enjoyed a brief tour of the city with Katz as a superb and well-informed guide. He'd seen the Wailing Wall, surrounded by such Islamic sites as the Dome of the Rock and the El Aqsa Mosque in the area known as Temple Mount, regarded by Muslims as the most important shrines after Mecca and Medina. The old synagogue area was found in the Jewish Quarter. The Church of the Redeemer, the Cathedral of St. James and the Spring of the Virgin could be clearly seen from Mount Zion and the Tomb of David.

Domes and steeples extended into the sky in every direction. Houses of worship for Jews, Muslims and Christians were found throughout the city. Yet these religions didn't coexist in harmony. Jerusalem had always been a prize everyone wanted. Since 1980 the entire city had been claimed by Israel as the nation's capital "for all time." This was unacceptable to many Arabs. Holy Jerusalem, like all of the Middle East, dwelled in the shadow of danger, threatened by violence and war.

"Mr. Pollock?" Moshin's voice called to the Executioner.

"Yeah," Bolan replied, turning from the window.

"Is something wrong? You seem to be looking outside with some intensity. If you're concerned that someone could use a laser microphone to eavesdrop on our conversations as we did at the warehouse, don't be worried. A system of metal rods is planted in the window frame to create a constant series of vibrations similar to a tuning fork. A laser mike won't detect any sounds except a low-pitched hum along the surface of the glass."

"I see," Bolan said with a nod. He didn't bother to explain his thoughts.

"The glass is also tinted on the outside," Moshin added. "This is to prevent anyone from using a telescope to peer into the office and read lips. We try to take every possible precaution for security."

"I'm impressed," Bolan assured him.

Moshin was seated at his desk, monitoring a computer terminal. Recent police and military reports appeared on the screen. The captain barely glanced at the information. None of it seemed connected to the Samson Warriors. More data replaced the reports, but Moshin didn't seem encouraged by what he saw.

"This is frustrating," Katz commented. He sat by another computer that was set up on a small table in Moshin's office. "We usually have other people who do this sort of technical data gathering. I'm not terribly happy with Geller's idea of cooperation.''

''Maybe you didn't make a very good impression when you met with the director,'' Bolan remarked. ''It sounds like he would have been more pleased with a detailed report on our mission. Especially if it had implicated Arab terrorism instead of actions committed by Israelis and American Jews.''

''He'd like the world to be black and white,'' Katz replied, ''good guys and bad guys clearly labeled, each side with a definite ideology one can either support or oppose. It's hard for Geller to see men who favor a strong Israel as villains, even if they're extremists who resort to violence against innocent civilians.''

''Don't be too hard on the director,'' Moshin urged. ''He supplied us with the computer contacts we requested. Geller would probably give us the extra operators to screen information if we could tell him precisely what we're looking for.''

''That's a problem,'' Bolan stated. ''We won't know what it is until we find it. The Samson Warriors are pretty unpredictable even by terrorist standards.''

Moshin looked at the computer screen. His face screwed into an expression of disgust, and he muttered something in Hebrew. Bolan asked what was wrong.

''I just read a rather disturbing police report concerning a violent assault on a young woman in Northern Galilee. I'm sure it has nothing to do with the Samson Warriors.''

"What sort of assault?" Bolan demanded.

"She was attacked on a road. A man stopped his car and attacked without provocation. He didn't rape her, but beat her badly. Flogged the poor woman."

"Flogged her?" Katz asked with interest. "Did the report state if her skin was torn by hooks as well as scourged?"

"It said her flesh was ripped, but didn't mention if hooks were used," Moshin answered, puzzled by Katz's question. "I don't see that this hideous incident has any connection with the Samson Warriors."

"There's a verse from the books of the Prophets," Katz began. He turned to Bolan. "As a non-Jew, you'd know it as part of the Old Testament. It's found in 1 Kings—'My father hath chastised you with whips, but I will chastise you with scorpions.' The scorpion it refers to is a scorpion whip. It resembled a cat-o'-nine-tails with metal hooks attached to the lashes."

"Pretty vicious instrument to use to punish someone," Bolan commented. "Just the sort of thing that would appeal to a demented sadist like Ezra Avriel."

"You think Avriel did this terrible thing?" Moshin asked with a frown. "Why would he attack an innocent woman?"

"Avriel has a history of assaulting women," the Executioner reminded the Mossad officer. "He spent time in a mental institute for beating women he thought were prostitutes. He probably enjoys 'punishing' women for their alleged sins. He might have jumped the female victim in Galilee and whipped her because he wanted to celebrate escaping from Tel Aviv after shooting into the crowd of potential Samson recruits at the rally.''

"This seems farfetched to me,'' Moshin said. "I believe you call it grasping for straws. The attack on the woman was certainly the act of a sadistic individual, but that doesn't mean Avriel did it. Northern Galilee is quite a long way from Tel Aviv.''

Katz checked a map of Israel on the wall. "Highway 11 extends north from Tel Aviv to Haifa,'' he announced. "Avriel could have easily driven along the coast from one city to the other.''

"It's the only lead we've got,'' Bolan added. "Maybe this is an unrelated incident, but we can't afford to ignore it. Let's check it out. Geller can find some people to monitor the computers in case some other suspicious reports come in from the police and military agencies.''

"He can certainly find someone better suited to run a computer than I am,'' Katz declared. "I'm more familiar with military hardware than computer software.''

"I'll talk to Geller,'' Moshin told his companions. "We'll have the computer technicians we need and transportation to Carmiel. That's the city where the police report about the woman came from.''

"Make it fast transport,'' Bolan insisted. "We can't allow the trail to go cold.''

LEVI BIRNBAUM WAS FURIOUS. His powerful fingers flexed into fists. The Samson leader was tempted to punch Ezra Avriel in his grinning face or even throttle him. Avriel had arrived at the Samson Warriors' new base and happily bragged about the sniper attack on the rally in Tel Aviv.

Chaim Stern shook his head as he listened to the man. Birnbaum avoided looking at Stern, who had warned him about Avriel, saying that he was too unstable to be part of a covert operation of any sort. Birnbaum realized Stern was right.

The Samson leader had known Avriel was insane, but he hadn't wanted to accept the fact. Avriel had been one of the first to join the Samson Warriors. His dedication to Birnbaum's dogma had been absolute, and he was willing to do anything, literally anything, for their cause. Since Birnbaum was a fanatic himself, he tended to overlook Avriel's mental condition and even excuse the madman's occasional assaults on women he considered to be prostitutes as an "overzealous expression of religious devotion."

However, Birnbaum had always realized Avriel enjoyed hurting women and that his religious beliefs had nothing to do with his vicious pastime. Avriel used the punishment excuse to justify beating women because he liked doing it. Now that the killing had started the man enjoyed that, as well. Birnbaum's old colleague was like an attack dog that had been overtrained. He was becoming too dangerous to trust on his own, and he might indeed become a threat to his fellow Samson Warriors.

In fact, the man might have already crossed that line. He wasn't a physical threat to Birnbaum's group, but his actions could have put the entire organization in jeopardy. Avriel didn't seem to comprehend this or suspect that he'd done anything that could endanger Birnbaum's plans.

"You shot several of our supporters because you believe one of them must have been an informer who told the authorities about the meetings at the warehouse," Stern said with a weary sigh. "What did you think this would accomplish? The CIA or the Mossad or whoever attacked the warehouse found our five missing comrades hidden there. They already knew everything the informer could have told them because we didn't reestablish contact with the new recruits. Why kill three or four potential recruits in order to take out one man who could no longer cause us any harm?"

"We can't allow enemies to go unpunished," Avriel declared proudly. "The informer was probably a Jew. That makes him a traitor to our people. Any Jew who fails to share our vision is a coward and an enemy. Besides, we must make examples of such opponents to show others how we deal with our enemies."

"Only one of the men you killed could have been the informer," Birnbaum stated. "The others were our allies and would have become loyal Samson Warriors had they lived."

"That is unfortunate," Avriel said with a shrug, "but necessary to be certain of killing the enemy agent. I'm sure God will understand and the young men will be welcomed in the next life. Meantime they serve us for the purpose of Samson martyrs. I told you I wore Arab clothing and used an AK-47 assault rifle. The Palestinians will be blamed for the shooting."

"I don't imagine anyone would suspect we're killing our own supporters," Stern commented, a trace of bitterness in his tone. "You were lucky, Ezra. Such a sniper attack without backup or assistance in the getaway or disposal of disguise and weapons was very risky."

"They weren't looking for an American Jew," Avriel said with a smile. "I strolled right past the police without any problem. No one suspected me for an instant."

"How did they know you were an American Jew?" Birnbaum demanded, alarm in his voice. "Did they simply recognize your accent and let you go?"

"I had to show them my passport, of course," Avriel admitted, "but they barely glanced at my ID and I easily bluffed my way through the few questions asked—"

"You didn't use your real passport?" Stern asked, worried that he would hear an affirmative reply.

Avriel confirmed his fears. "Of course I did. God protected me."

"God might be helping the people stalking us by making you behave like an idiot," Stern growled.

Avriel's expression suddenly changed. His eyes blazed with anger and his lips curled back into a snarl. He pivoted and crossed the room to a duffel bag he'd placed in a corner. The guy wasn't carrying a gun, and the others assumed he was headed for the bag to grab a weapon. Stern immediately drew a Beretta pistol from leather, but Birnbaum stepped between the two men.

"Put the gun away," the Samson leader ordered.

"You keep your animal on a leash," Stern replied, but he raised the pistol to point the muzzle at the ceiling.

Birnbaum turned to Avriel, who had taken an odd instrument from his duffel bag. He held it by a wooden handle and nine leather straps unwound from the grips. Steel hooks studded the lashes. Birnbaum noticed that the metal and leather were stained with half-dried blood.

"This son of a bitch insulted me!" Avriel hissed, raising the whip. "I will teach him some respect with my scorpion."

"Where did you get that thing?" Birnbaum demanded, still blocking Avriel's path to Stern. "Looks like you already used it on someone."

"I made the scorpion whip myself," the man replied proudly. "I encountered a harlot on the road and gave her a taste of the lash for her sins."

"My God," Birnbaum said, shaking his head. "What have you done, Ezra?"

"You're upset because I punished a whore?" Avriel asked, genuinely confused by the other man's reaction. "I'm just obeying the word of God, Levi."

"I doubt you can find any scriptures to prove that," Stern remarked. "Yet it might not be so bad. We were already burned after the warehouse was raided. The warning that we couldn't return to the kibbutz outside Tel Aviv was proof of that. The authorities were looking for everyone associated with the Samson Warriors before this incident. Ezra was lucky they didn't recognize his name when the police stopped him. Most likely the city police hadn't been informed about us by the Mossad, the CIA or whoever's after the Samson Warriors."

"Even Chaim admits I did nothing wrong," Avriel said cheerfully. "There's nothing to worry about, Levi."

"I'd say our briefing is over, Ezra," Birnbaum replied. "Go to your quarters and get some rest. We'll speak later."

Avriel tucked the scorpion whip under an arm and gathered up his duffel bag. The other men waited for him to leave the house before they spoke. Stern checked the door to be certain Avriel wasn't trying to eavesdrop outside the building. He watched as the twisted American strolled across the kibbutz to a row of small houses, then locked the door and turned to face Birnbaum. "You have to get rid of him, Levi."

"I don't need to hear you say 'I told you so,'" Birnbaum replied. "It's obvious Ezra has become a problem."

"When I said it wasn't so bad that Avriel flashed his passport to the police, I was lying," Stern stated. "That maniac destroyed the value of his ruthless sniper attack because the authorities will soon learn he was at the site of the shooting and realize the gunman was Ezra, not an Arab killer. No propaganda advantage was gained by that stunt. Ezra might not have even killed the informer...if there was an informer."

"Do you think he jeopardized our base here?" Birnbaum asked as he moved across the room to pick up a dumbbell. "Could he have been tracked here somehow?"

"Possibly. Not very likely. Attacking that woman won't help our position. Hopefully no one will connect the assault with Avriel. Better find out where he attacked the woman. If it was done near Tel Aviv, it won't help the authorities place us in Northern Galilee."

"What if he did it in this district?" Birnbaum asked. "Let's consider the worst possibility. How long will it take the Mossad or whoever to find us?"

"A local criminal case handled by the police probably won't be noticed by Jerusalem for a few days," Stern answered. "I don't know if they have Avriel's criminal history on file, but the CIA might and they'll probably assist the Mossad. They might put two and two together in less than a week. Of course, they'll expect us to move to another kibbutz because we used one as a base outside Tel Aviv, but it will take some time to locate the right one.''

"Then we have to make our next move soon," Birnbaum declared. "Circumstances have offered us an ideal target. I think you know what I'm talking about. We discussed it earlier."

"I know what you mean," Stern said with a frown. "We also agreed he'd be a very difficult target. Personally I'd be delighted to kill him, but many have tried in the past. He's not an easy man to kill."

"But it would certainly force the Arab world into making a move against Israel. The Palestinians would definitely respond. That would force Israel into taking the sort of strong offensive actions necessary to become a powerful nation."

"It could trigger a full-scale war between Israel and one or more Arab nations. Israel can surely win such a conflict. Our military is greater than any of the Arab countries, and they're divided among themselves. However, the Arabs might unite and organize to fight Israel."

"They couldn't even organize and agree to action against Iraq when it invaded Kuwait and threatened Saudi Arabia and the other Gulf States," Birnbaum stated. "The United States will support Israel if we can start a war now. Despite criticism in the States, America will still back Israel. That could change in the future. Ezra might have done us a favor by making it necessary for us to take more drastic action."

"At least we won't be shedding more Israeli blood," Stern said with a sigh. "Not directly, that is. What about Avriel? I think it's obvious that we can't trust him on a mission as critical as this."

"No, we can't," Birnbaum admitted, raising the dumbbell overhead. His powerful arm moved back and bent at the elbow in a series of French curls.

"I think we should execute Ezra," Stern announced in a firm voice. "He's insane and a constant threat to our plans."

"But he's loyal, and he'll do what I tell him to as long as others are on hand to control him," Birnbaum stated. "It was a mistake to let him go on his own when the rest of us abandoned the Tel Aviv site and headed here. I'll assign him to security duty here at the kibbutz along with enough people to keep him in line."

"We'll need our best people for the next phase of our mission," Stern warned. "Don't leave anyone as Ezra's watchdog whom we might need when we cross into Lebanon."

"I know," Birnbaum assured him. "We'll pick the best qualified Israeli and American members. The rest can stay here and supply support in an emergency if we get into trouble in the field."

"They might not be able to help us," Stern said grimly, "but I suppose no one will be able to help Munir Kmed, either."

12

Lyova Tuvim lay in a hospital bed, her body wrapped in bandages. The woman's face and head hadn't been scarred or bruised by the brutal ordeal that had left her torso and limbs battered, torn and bloodied. Pain formed lines in her pretty features.

"My patient has suffered considerable physical injury and even more severe psychological trauma," the doctor told Katz and Captain Moshin as they stood by the threshold to Lyova's room. "The police have already questioned her, and she's had far more stress than any injured person should have to endure."

"We wouldn't be here unless it was urgent, Doctor," Katz assured him. The Phoenix commander glanced at the slim figure in the bed. "I'm afraid we have to talk to her now. This simply can't wait."

"Do you realize what happened to that poor woman?" the doctor demanded. "Whoever attacked her flogged her and ripped strips of flesh from her back, abdomen, breasts, arms and legs. Miss Tuvim is only twenty years old. She'll undergo a long series of operations. Mostly plastic surgery, but she'll still carry many of those scars for the rest of her life."

"You don't want the man who did this to attack another young lady, do you?" Moshin said. "I'm sure she wants him captured, as well."

"You showed me the Mossad identification," the doctor said, staring hard at the captain's face. "Why is your organization interested in an assault on a woman by a deranged sadist? He wouldn't happen to be one of your men who is out of control, would he?"

"That's an outrageous remark," Moshin replied, offended by the suggestion.

"With soldiers behaving like butchers during the *intifadeh* I wouldn't say it's impossible the Mossad might have a madman or two in its ranks," the doctor said with a shrug.

"The man we seek isn't a Mossad agent," Katz assured the doctor, "but it's a matter of national security, so we can't give you any details except to say the man is an enemy of everything decent people believe in. He's wanted for murder and several other crimes."

"Very well," the doctor reluctantly agreed. "Speak with Miss Tuvim, but keep it brief. Don't upset her more than necessary. Bear in mind her physical condition and show a little compassion for what she's been through."

"Thank you, Doctor," Katz said with a nod.

Lyova wasn't pleased to see yet another pair of strangers approach her bed. The young woman had spent the past three hours being probed and examined by medical personnel she'd never met before. She'd been questioned by police officers already. This pair didn't seem to be police, but Lyova guessed they were authorities of some kind.

More questions, she guessed, more implications that she had somehow provoked the attack. The police had asked her if she knew her assailant. Was he a jealous lover? A neighbor whom she had become friendly with? Had she done anything to encourage violence? Was she dressed in a provocative manner or did she flirt with the man? Was she hitchhiking and behaving in a tempting fashion to lure passing motorists to stop and offer a ride?

She expected another round of such questions. The younger man looked tough and physically fit. His hair was clipped short, and his neatly pressed khaki shirt and pants resembled a uniform. Highly shined low-quarters confirmed her suspicion that he was in the military. The older man was less formal in appearance. His eyes were gentle and wise. The elder's lips adopted a sad smile. He seemed sympathetic. Lyova noticed the artificial arm and realized the man was no stranger to suffering.

"We're sorry to disturb you," Katz said gently. "We'll try to make this brief and let you get some badly needed rest."

"I've already told the police everything I know," she replied in a tired voice. "I never met the man before. I didn't tease him or suggest any sexual favors.

He didn't even attempt any sexual advances or rape for that matter."

"That fits the profile of the man we believe to be your attacker," Moshin told her. "Do you think you'd recognize him?"

"I'll never forget his face," she confirmed. "Have you arrested him? I'll gladly press charges."

"We haven't caught him yet," Katz explained, "but you might be able to help us find the man. First, we need to know if he's the same person we've been hunting."

Moshin produced a photograph of Ezra Avriel from the mug shots taken by police in the United States. Lyova immediately recognized the man's face and confirmed that Avriel had been the one who'd assaulted her on the road.

"Who is he?" she asked. Lyova started to sit up in the bed, but the pain in her back forced her to lie still.

"A very sick individual with a history of violent attacks against women in America," Moshin explained.

"American?" she asked with a frown. "That explains why he spoke English. I'm not fluent in the language, so I can't tell you exactly what he said."

"That isn't important," Katz stated. "The ravings of a lunatic aren't worth recording regardless of the language. I understand you were on foot when the attack occurred. Avriel was in a vehicle, correct? Can you describe it?"

"A yellow car," she answered. "The word Toyota was printed on the side. A Japanese import, I think."

"You didn't notice a license plate number?" Moshin asked.

"I'm afraid not," she replied dryly. "I was busy trying to get away from him, then simply trying to survive when the bastard used a whip on me."

"That's understandable," Katz assured her. "Do you recall which way the car was headed when he stopped the vehicle and attacked you?"

"North," Lyova answered with a frown. "Was he running away from you people?"

"Something like that," Katz said. "And we don't want him to get any farther. That means we have to leave now. Thank you for your help. We'll let you know when we catch the man."

"Just get him," she urged, her eyes burning with anger. "No one should be allowed to get away with what he did to me."

"No one gets away from us."

CARMIEL WASN'T MUCH of a tourist attraction, which was okay with the Executioner. Mack Bolan had waited at a hangar of the small airstrip where the Bell chopper had landed outside the city. He spent the time checking weapons and other gear and maintained radio contact with Mossad headquarters in Jerusalem. Bolan was in danger of being bored when Katz and Moshin returned in the Jeep.

"Good news," Katz announced as he emerged from the vehicle. "We spoke with the injured woman, and she confirmed that Avriel was the man who attacked her. She also gave us a description of his car."

"A yellow Toyota Corolla," Bolan said with a nod. "I wrote down the license number, as well."

"How did you learn this?" Moshin asked, astonished.

"I spoke with Sergeant Goldberg, the guy in charge of the computer jockeys back at Mossad HQ," Bolan explained. "I had him run a check with the car rental outfits in Tel Aviv to see if Avriel had rented a car. I figured if the man was careless enough to show his passport to the police in Tel Aviv, he might be stupid enough to use his real name to rent a car."

"Incredible," the Mossad captain said, shaking his head slightly. "I just assumed Avriel must have stolen a car."

"I should have guessed he'd use a rental agency," Katz remarked with a sigh. "The man's a fanatic and fancies himself to be some sort of avenger of God's word. That's why he attacked Miss Tuvim and accused her of being a prostitute. Of course, all the Samson Warriors are fanatics, but Avriel is probably the only one who appears to believe God is personally protecting his every move. Such a man would never steal a car."

"Just to be on the safe side I had them contact the Tel Aviv police and run a check on recently stolen cars," Bolan commented. "Avriel seems to be able to justify ignoring the commandment concerning 'thou shalt not kill,' so I thought he might have decided to ignore the one about stealing, as well.''

"Obviously he chose the rental agency instead," Moshin said. "But you couldn't have been sure Avriel was the man who attacked Lyova Tuvim."

"We suspected this was more than a coincidence or we wouldn't have come here," Bolan stated. "The computer checks on the rentals and stolen cars were just a way to cover all possibilities. Avriel sure as hell needed transportation to get from Tel Aviv to Carmiel. Yakov even mentioned what route he might have used to drive here."

"And it's unlikely he would have taken a plane or train to Northern Galilee and then gotten a car somehow," Moshin said, following Bolan's logic.

"Actually he could have traveled to Haifa and rented a car there," the Executioner said with a shrug. "That's not important. What matters is we've got a positive ID on Avriel and we know he's in this district. Maybe now we'll get lucky with police reports or information from gas stations in the area."

"What's this?" Katz inquired.

"Another thing I told Goldberg to check on," the Executioner explained. "After I found out the type of car and the license plate number, I told him to have an all-points bulletin issued by the police in this district. I said I wanted them to keep track of where the car is headed, but not to close in or try to arrest Avriel."

"Good idea," Moshin agreed. "How do gas stations apply? No! Wait. I see it now. Avriel can't drive across half of Israel without stopping to get gasoline somewhere along the way. You think of everything, Mr. Pollock."

"That's why he's the best," Katz said, also impressed with Bolan's mental legwork. "We can limit that area now. Avriel was headed north when he attacked the woman. That means he's gone somewhere between Carmiel and the Lebanese border."

"That's a long way from the West Bank and the *intifadeh*," Bolan remarked. "If Avriel's planning to join Birnbaum and the others, the Samson Warriors must have a reason for setting up camp in Northern Galilee."

"Maybe it's just a temporary base far from where they were stationed before due to contacts within the Israeli sympathizers of the terrorist outfit," Moshin suggested. "They might yet plan to carry out more hit-and-run attacks to stir up the *intifadeh*."

"Maybe," the Executioner replied. "Birnbaum might decide to lay low for a while or to move on to whatever he plans to do next."

"He probably had to change his plans radically after our raid on the warehouse," Katz reminded Bolan.

"Yeah, but I don't think he's the type to stay put for long. The Samsons have been busy since they arrived in Israel. My guess is they'll try to carry out another operation as soon as possible. We forced them to abandon their base in Tel Aviv, but Birnbaum might just read that as a signal to pull off his next attack before we can locate him again."

"Then I hope we find them soon," Moshin said grimly. "The terrorists have been partially successful. The *intifadeh* has become worse, and Israel is getting a lot of flak from Arab nations for the violence triggered by the Samson Warriors' attack in the West Bank. I hate to think what Birnbaum might try next. Even Avriel's lunatic sniping accomplished at least one goal. Lieutenant Yarok was killed, and the shooting has outraged Israelis who still believe the gunman was an Arab. It probably even increased support for the Samson Warriors and Birnbaum's position that Israel take a more offensive posture."

"'For I will gather all nations against Jerusalem to battle,'" Katz declared. "That's from the last chapter of Zechariah. It speaks of the last days and the final judgment by God. If Israel becomes more aggressive, it could indeed lead to war with all the Arab nations. Of course, Jerusalem is the capital of Israel."

"You don't think that Birnbaum is somehow carrying out actions to make that prophecy come to pass?" Moshin asked, staring at Katz in astonishment."

"I certainly hope not, but Birnbaum might think so."

"If God wants to end the world, that's one thing," the Executioner stated. "But if the Samson Warriors want to get a war started with acts of murder and terrorism, that's quite another. Birnbaum is going to have his own personal judgment day when we find him.''

13

The kibbutz appeared tranquil as Mack Bolan scanned the farming community with a pair of binoculars. Twilight descended upon the collection of small houses and diminutive crops of wheat and corn. A man sat on a porch, cleaning and oiling a disassembled Galil rifle. Bolan recognized the guy's face. He'd seen Ezra Avriel's mug shot enough in the past eight hours to be able to confirm a positive ID.

"Looks like we hit the jackpot this time," the Executioner announced as he lowered the binoculars.

The Mossad investigation, orchestrated by Bolan, had discovered a gas station attendant who remembered an American "who spoke Hebrew poorly" and drove a yellow Toyota. Since tourists seldom ventured to Northern Galilee and almost never traveled so close to the Lebanese border, the attendant vividly remembered the guy. The same man also recalled that three trucks loaded with women, children, a couple of elderly men, furniture and bags of personal belongings had also purchased gasoline earlier the same day. The attendant had overheard one of the older passengers complaining about being driven out of their homes to make room for a bunch of foreigners.

The guy at the gas station had wondered if the two incidents were connected because he'd suspected the crowded trucks had come from a kibbutz located between Hurfeish and Fassuta. The American in the Toyota could have been one of the foreigners the old man had complained about, the attendant figured.

The man was right on the money with his deductions. In Bolan's opinion the attendant was too sharp to be pumping gas for a living.

The police at Hurfeish had also noticed the family members from the kibbutz when they arrived in the town. Hurfeish was close enough to the kibbutz for the townspeople to know something about the people living at the commune. They were clanlike and had little to do with the neighboring towns, yet the limited contact with Hurfeish revealed the kibbutz population consisted of a small number of families and unmarried young men with radical views about Israel as the dominant force in the Middle East.

The collection of evidence clearly indicated that the kibbutz was a Samson base. Captain Moshin contacted Geller and called for backup. Bolan insisted that the Mossad send only a few commandos because a large unit of men arriving in the area would draw unwanted attention. The Samson Warriors had supporters among the general population throughout Israel. If a sympathizer spotted a group of gunships or troop transport trucks headed for the kibbutz, a radio message or phone call could alert Birnbaum. The terrorists would certainly flee if they suspected a raid was imminent.

Half a dozen Israeli paratroopers arrived in a Bell chopper at the airstrip near Carmiel. Clad in combat fatigues and red berets, the soldiers were armed with grenades, assault rifles and machine guns, and were ready for action.

Bolan, Katz and Moshin met the paratroopers at the airstrip and briefly explained the situation and strategy involved. Three civilian automobiles were supplied by the Carmiel police, thanks to Moshin's Mossad authority. The Executioner personally elected to take point and to scout the kibbutz. He wanted Katz and Moshin to remain with the paratroopers to assume command in case he didn't return.

Lieutenant Levitch, the team leader of the Israeli troops, volunteered to accompany Bolan. The young officer spoke English fluently and had combat experience as an antiterrorist against Palestinian extremist outfits in the 1980s. The warrior reluctantly agreed to let Levitch come with him, handing the man the keys to the car chosen for the point vehicle.

They drove ten miles to Hurfeish, parked a little less than a mile from the kibbutz and approached on foot.

Bolan carried his M-16 with M-203 attachment, as well as the Beretta 93-R and Desert Eagle pistols. He was also armed with grenades, garrotes and Ka-bar fighting knife. Yet this was a recon operation and Bolan didn't want a confrontation with the Samson

Warriors. Levitch was also heavily armed and understood that the purpose of the soft probe was to acquire information without bloodshed.

The Executioner crawled to a ridge and studied the kibbutz with his binoculars. The discovery of Ezra Avriel confirmed that they had found the Samson lair. Other men were present at the kibbutz, and all were armed and appeared nervous. Bolan could only guess how many Samson Warriors were inside the small houses. Two large military trucks were parked in the area, and he also spotted Avriel's rented Toyota and two other automobiles.

"I wish we had more men," Levitch whispered to Bolan. "We'll surely be outnumbered when we launch the raid on this kibbutz."

"We have to play the game with the hand we've been dealt," the Executioner replied, returning the binoculars to a carrying case. "Let's get out of here. We've seen enough to form a plan to take the place."

"It had better be a very good plan," Levitch commented. "There are only nine of us, including your one-armed friend who appears to be too old for this sort of thing."

The Executioner favored the commando with a hard stare. "My 'one-armed friend' isn't here because he's a charity case."

"I hope you know what you're doing, Mr. Pollock," the lieutenant remarked, a trace of doubt in his voice.

"We'll find out soon enough," Bolan replied as they crept from the ridge to head back to the car.

THE STRIKE FORCE HEADED toward the kibbutz one hour later. The plan was simple. They formed a broken horseshoe formation to cover the commune from three sides. Lieutenant Levitch led two men to the position on the ridge. Katz commanded two paratroopers and moved to the western flank. Bolan, Moshin and an NCO named Segal headed east.

The approach was slow and stealthy. Bolan correctly assumed that sentries would be posted after sundown. Two men marched along the perimeter of the kibbutz on the eastern and western flanks. They carried assault rifles and flashlights. Both guards appeared to be alert and especially concerned with the ridge overlooking the commune, correctly recognizing it as the most vulnerable area for the security of the base because it offered the best concealment for possible invaders.

Damn right. That was why Levitch and two other commandos were positioned on the ridge. The sentries paid more attention to the obvious threat to the safety of their camp than to the rest of the surroundings. This was in the favor of Bolan and his allies, but there was little natural cover on either the western or eastern flanks. Lights in the windows of all but one house revealed that the buildings were occupied and at least some of the men within were still awake.

Bolan was glad the Samson Warriors had evacuated the women, children and elderly from the kibbutz—no innocent bystanders to worry about. The fact that the terrorists had moved their families from the site revealed concern for the safety of loved ones. However, the Samsons had shown little regard for innocent lives that weren't blood relatives of the Israeli members of the fanatic outfit. So much for humanitarian kudos to a gang of mad dogs.

The Executioner handed his M-16 to Captain Moshin. He needed to dispatch the sentry on the eastern flank as silently as possible. A single gunshot would alert the Samson forces inside the dwellings. Bolan trusted Katz and the men under his command to take care of the other guard. He crept from the cover of a sparse bush and moved into the shadows along the perimeter of the kibbutz.

Clad in black, face and hands smeared with night combat cosmetics, Bolan once again melted into the darkness. He kept his knees bent and his back hunched low, head bowed below the shoulder line so that he didn't provide a clear human outline among the shadows.

The guard started to turn from the ridge and walked toward the Executioner's position. Bolan froze in place. He knew that a figure close to the ground was difficult to see in the dark unless a man was looking for it. The sentry didn't appear to sense Bolan's presence as he walked in a straight line along the perimeter. The sentry carried a Galil across a shoulder in a casual manner, but Bolan's hand remained poised on the grips of the Beretta holstered under his arm.

The throbbing of the pulse behind Bolan's ear sounded like enemy footsteps closing in from the rear. The big warrior was familiar with stress and didn't move his head or take his eyes away from the guard. The guy continued to stroll past the warrior's position and even took a pack of cigarettes from a shirt pocket, unaware of the danger that lurked less than three yards away.

Bolan had to take down the man fast, which he could do in a thousand different ways. He didn't want to kill the guy, but he recalled the fight with another sentry at the Tel Aviv warehouse. It was likely that all the Samson Warriors were trained in hand-to-hand combat. Birnbaum was a muscle boy and probably insisted his men practice physical fitness. If he slugged the guard, Bolan would have to bring him down with one blow.

The sputtering cough of a silenced weapon suddenly broke the silence. Bolan heard a soft moan and a body strike the ground, but he kept his attention fixed on the guard. The sentry spun, startled by the noise. He swung the Galil from his shoulder, but Bolan's Beretta had already cleared leather. One 9 mm round drilled into the sentry and sent him stumbling backward, the rifle slipping from the man's grasp as he died on his feet. A well-placed Parabellum bullet had punched into an eye socket and exited at the back of the man's skull.

The Executioner glanced around and saw Katz on the western flank. The Phoenix Force veteran carried a Walther P-88 with a nine-inch silencer, and he appeared to be annoyed. Bolan noticed the second guard lay dead near the one-armed commando's feet. The sentry had obviously discovered Katz, and the Phoenix pro had taken him out with the pistol.

So it could have gone better, Bolan thought, but it could have been a hell of a lot worse. The warrior headed for the bush where Moshin and Segal were waiting. He heard the hinges of a door creak, and light suddenly spilled across his body.

Bolan turned and saw a figure standing in a doorway. He barely glimpsed the pistol in the guy's hand as he snap-aimed the 93-R and triggered two rounds. Nine-millimeter messengers of death nailed the Samson fanatic in the chest and ripped through his heart and lungs. The man fell backward into the room as startled voices inside the house shouted with alarm when they saw bloodied bullet holes in their comrade's shirt.

So much for the soft probe, Bolan thought fleetingly as he threw himself to the ground and rolled to the side of the house. Glass shattered from a window above his prone form. He glanced up and saw a rifle barrel poke through the opening. Bolan's silenced Beretta hadn't alerted the entire kibbutz, but there was no doubt everyone in the house was aware that the Samsons were under attack. Soon the terrorists in the other dwellings would also know.

Bolan thumbed the selector to 3-round bursts and pointed the 93-R at the doorway. Two shapes appeared on the threshold, weapons in hand. A trio of 9 mm slugs from the Beretta struck the gunner closer to the warrior and pitched him backward into the path of his companion. The Executioner fell to one knee as he blasted the second gunman with another burst from the Beretta.

The rifle barrel shifted across the windowsill above Bolan. The gunman at the window was trying to locate him, but he didn't realize how close the Executioner was. Bolan swiftly grabbed the barrel and yanked forcibly. The terrorist was abruptly pulled forward, his head and shoulders smashing through what remained of the windowpane. The Executioner chopped the butt of his Beretta into the man's temple. The Samson Warrior slumped across the windowsill, out of the fight.

The Executioner grabbed the Galil with one hand, the other fisted around the butt of the 93-R, raced to the end of the wall and swung around the corner. A burst of bullets tore chunks from the house as Bolan reached cover. The warrior hastily holstered the Beretta and grasped the Galil with both hands. He would have been more comfortable with his M-16, but Bolan was no stranger to the Galil.

The Israeli assault rifle was similar in design to the Soviet Kalashnikov, but with a few additional features. Bolan wasn't interested in the folding carrying handle between the foregrip and bolt or the built-in wire cutter section of the bipod attachment to the barrel. However, he made certain the flip-up illuminated front sight was in place for night use and the L-type aperture to the rear sight was up. He locked the folding stock in place and worked the cocking knob. Although it was unlikely the terrorist had wielded the weapon without chambering a round, Bolan couldn't be sure he had a cartridge under the firing pin unless he made certain of that himself.

A shell hopped from the chamber, so the precaution had been unnecessary. At least he knew the weapon was ready for action as the bolt fed another round home. The magazine was a short model for a Galil. That meant it had a 35-round capacity, but Bolan had ejected one shell and didn't know how many 5.56 mm cartridges had been loaded into the magazine by the Samson Warrior.

Whatever the ammo count was, Bolan could use the extra firepower. The numbers were falling fast, and the Executioner was armed and ready.

AFTER SHOTS WERE finally fired by a weapon without a silencer, the entire kibbutz was alerted to danger. Samson terrorists emerged from houses, expecting to encounter an army of opponents. They were confused and unaware of where the raiders were located until automatic rifles erupted from the Israeli paratroopers surrounding the kibbutz. Bullets slashed into several Samson Warriors, propelling them to the ground in thrashing heaps. Others bolted for cover.

The Samsons returned fire, aiming at the muzzle-flash of the soldiers' assault weapons.

Bolan was in a tight position. He had to stay low to avoid friendly fire from the paratroopers and to cope with the terrorists at the same time. He crawled on elbows and knees to the rear of the house, the Galil rifle cradled in the crooks of his elbows. Bullets raked the walls of the building as he moved to the new position, adobe dust showering his back and hair. Dirt splattered his clothes as slugs struck the ground near his body. The Executioner clenched his teeth and kept moving.

He reached the rear of the house and found two Samson Warriors literally slipping out the back door. Bolan raised the Galil and opened fire. A 3-round burst punched one opponent under the rib cage, the 5.56 mm projectiles slicing upward to churn liver and gall bladder into useless tissue.

The Samson Warrior collapsed as his comrade whirled and fired an Uzi submachine gun in Bolan's general direction. The second guy was quick. Too quick. He failed to take time to aim. The 9 mm slugs sizzled above Bolan as he remained prone and triggered the Galil to blast the machine gunner through the heart.

The warrior plucked a grenade from his belt and pulled the pin. He popped the spoon and held the M-26 blaster in one fist and the Galil in the other. He allowed two tense seconds to pass for the timing mechanism of the grenade fuse to reach a critical point before he lobbed the orb through the open doorway of the house.

The grenade sailed past the face of another Samson Warrior who had decided to investigate the gunshots at the rear of the building. He was distracted by the sphere and turned his head away from Bolan. The Executioner swung the Galil toward the terrorist, fist around the pistol grip and the buttstock braced on a hip. He fired the rifle and pumped three rounds into the side of the guy's skull. Another Samson Warrior fell, and Bolan ran for cover at the next building.

A terrorist outside the second building spotted the tall American and raised his weapon. Bolan was faster, and his accuracy remained precise and deadly. He fired the Galil on the run and sent the gunman to the ground in a wild convulsion of death. The Executioner dived forward, hit the ground in a shoulder roll and slid beside his slain opponent. He grabbed the guy and used the body for a shield as the grenade exploded inside the first house.

The blast burst windows and sent Samson extremists hurtling from the building, their bodies bloodied and mangled. Dismembered limbs, brutally amputated, lay among the debris from the blast. Cracks formed in the adobe walls as the entire building trembled from the force of the eruption.

Bits of stone and mortar pelted Bolan's position. The Executioner held the dead man toward the explosion in case the grenade detonated volatile material that might be stored in the house. The M-26 blast didn't cause such a reaction, and Bolan didn't need the lifeless human shield for protection. Yet, as he began to push the corpse aside and rise, he heard footfalls approach. Two Samson Warriors had stepped from the second house and saw the fireworks next door.

"God Almighty!" one of the terrorists exclaimed. "They blew up the fuckin' house!"

"And Eli's been injured," the other man added. His accent suggested he was an Israeli.

Bolan guessed Eli was the dead man who lay across his chest. The terrorist pair had noticed the corpse, but failed to detect Bolan beneath it. The Executioner's movement had been mistaken as that of the slain Eli. The men would soon realize their mistake when they got a better look at their "injured" comrade.

The Executioner had discarded the confiscated Galil rifle to use both hands when he moved the corpse as a shield. He shoved the body aside with one hand and reached for the holstered Beretta. The familiar pistol cleared leather smoothly. Even housed in the special oversize holster designed to accommodate the silencer as well as the 93-R, the weapon came free swiftly.

The muffled raspings of the silenced weapon belied the destructive power of the 9 mm slugs that split the Samson goon's breastbone and drilled a lethal tunnel in the guy's throat. The Israeli gunman started to point his weapon at Bolan as his comrade crumpled to the ground. The Executioner's pistol spit Parabellum death before the other man could trigger his assault rifle. The terrorist's face burst from a trio of bullets that chopped off his nose and punctured his forehead.

Movement drew Bolan's attention to a shape that materialized beside him, and the Stony Man fighting machine swung the Beretta toward the trouser-clad legs. A boot lashed out to kick the 93-R from the Executioner's hand. The face of his attacker loomed overhead, features contorted into an animal expression of fury and blood lust.

The terrorist's left arm hung useless, shattered by a pair of rifle rounds fired by the paratroopers surrounding the base. His right arm hadn't been injured, and the blade of a stiletto jutted from his fist. Although racked with pain, his face glazed with sweat, the man's eyes were filled with hatred and determination as he lunged, the knife aimed at Bolan's throat.

14

The Executioner shifted away from the attacker and pivoted on the small of his back. The stiletto missed Bolan's neck by less than an inch. The knife stabbed sand, and Bolan grabbed the guy's wrist before he could pull the blade free.

The warrior held his enemy's wrist to pin down the fist with the stiletto and slammed a knee kick at the terrorist's ribs. The Stony Man soldier's free hand grabbed the handle of the Ka-bar sheathed upside down on his harness. He drew the fighting knife and struck with a continuous fluid movement. The steel tip plunged into the side of the terrorist's neck, slitting his carotid artery and jugular. Blood jetted from the terrible wound and sprayed Bolan's sleeve as he carved across the terrorist's throat to cut the thyroid cartilage. The Samson Warrior was thrown into shock by the massive damage. His brain had already shut down before he died scant seconds later.

The Executioner retrieved the Beretta and returned the Ka-bar to its scabbard. He prepared to gather up the discarded Galil rifle as another terrorist appeared at the corner of the building by the front of the house. The Samson Warriors were coming out of the figurative woodwork like human cockroaches. Bolan aimed the Beretta at the unsuspecting gunner. The man's body suddenly jerked in a violent spasm as bullet holes blossomed liquid scarlet in the terrorist's chest.

Bolan watched the man fall and turned to see Captain Moshin and Sergeant Segal rush toward his position. The other members of the assault team directed their fire away from the eastern flank to avoid hitting Bolan or the two Israeli allies. Moshin jogged to the Executioner and tossed the M-16 to him.

"You might want this back," the captain stated as he grasped his own Galil rifle with both hands.

"Yeah. Thanks." Bolan worked the charging handle to the M-16 and chambered the first round.

He was finally able to take stock of the battle beyond his own personal efforts to survive. The Samson Warriors were losing the conflict thanks to the cunning and skill of Bolan and his temporary teammates. Lieutenant Levitch and his men on the ridge had set up the light machine gun to spray the terrorists with superior firepower. Katz had ordered the men under his command to fire their MK-19 launchers, but he wanted the 40 mm projectiles set off between buildings.

Although the assault force wasn't pulling any punches, the team didn't want to slaughter the Samson Warriors or level the kibbutz to the ground. They needed evidence that would confirm beyond any doubt that Birnbaum's outfit was responsible for the wave of terrorism that had shaken the state of Israel. They also wanted to take as many terrorists alive as possible for interrogation.

The grenade shells exploded within the camp on the western flank. A blast near one house showered it with dirt and shrapnel. At least one Samson gunman was blown to bits by the grenade because he had made the error of seeking cover along the side of the building. There might have been more than one victim of the blast. The chunks of human remains had been torn into fragments too small to be readily identified as belonging to a single person.

Another round missed the intended mark and hit the roof of a house. The explosion shattered the rooftop and smashed an entire wall from the building. Half the house caved in on the terrorists inside. Two Samson fighters bolted from the building, panicked by the unexpected attack. The pair didn't get far before machine gun fire from the FALO blaster on the ridge cut them down.

The battle was far from over, and it could still swing in favor of the Samson Warriors. Bolan's unit had the element of surprise and well-organized strategy when they hit the kibbutz. The enemy wasn't given an opportunity to form an organized and coordinated counterattack, but the Samsons were fanatics and might use a self-destruct device if they realized they didn't have a chance. A powerful explosive charge could destroy the entire camp. This suicidal tactic would wipe out the terrorists and probably take out some of the assault team, as well.

Bolan, Moshin and Segal were in the center of the kibbutz and prime candidates to be blown to oblivion if such a doomsday contraption was employed by the Samson Warriors. The Executioner didn't dwell on this danger. He gestured for Moshin and Segal to cover the front and rear entrances to the nearest house. When the Israeli commandos assumed their positions, Bolan tossed a concussion grenade through a shattered window.

Terrorists attempted to flee the building. Moshin and Segal forced the enemy to remain inside by simply firing a few full-auto rounds at each doorway. The Samson Warriors were trapped within the walls of the house when the grenade exploded. The concussion blast shook the dwelling and shattered glass from the two windows that had survived the previous assault.

"That should take care of everyone inside," Bolan announced, "but some of them might be only stunned. Don't get careless."

Moshin and Segal entered the building while Bolan turned his attention to a trio of Samson Warriors who suddenly broke cover and ran to the trucks and cars. Bolan swung his M-16 toward the opponents and fired. One terrorist was struck in the ribs and chest. He whirled from the impact of the 5.56 mm slugs and slammed into the side of the yellow Toyota. The man's corpse slid to the ground as his comrades attempted to return fire while still jogging for the cover of the vehicles.

Bolan had dropped to one knee and kept his M-16 trained on his adversaries. Bullets kicked up dirt near the Executioner, but his hands remained steady. The gunmen had reached the vehicles and didn't present a clear target.

"Not good enough," Bolan rasped, triggering the M-203 launcher.

The recoil jarred the M-16 buttstock into Bolan's shoulder forcibly. The 40 mm M-203 shell rocketed into the collection of trucks and cars and exploded, tearing the vehicles apart with the blast. Gasoline ignited, and flaming debris spread across the terrorists' motor pool. Fuel tanks blew, and more explosions sent chunks of burning wreckage in all directions. Pieces landed on the rooftops of nearby houses and set them ablaze. Bolan didn't see the two men who had ducked behind the vehicles, but he knew there would be little left of their bodies. The flames leaped from the improvised funeral pyre and cast ghastly yellow light across the kibbutz.

Moshin emerged from the doorway and stared at the burning destruction with astonishment. Terrorists emerged from two buildings, hands raised in surrender. They coughed violently and stumbled around, blinded by the dense smoke. They'd been trapped inside the burning houses and elected to give up rather than be cremated.

"Did you find anyone inside, Captain?" Bolan asked.

"Two live terrorists," Moshin replied. "Segal has them bound and held at gunpoint."

"Get them outside and be ready to round up the other prisoners when the shooting stops," Bolan instructed. "Get Levitch on the walkie-talkie. Tell him to watch where his people fire that FALO machine gun. We want as many of these Samson guys alive as possible."

"He knows that already."

"Remind him, anyway," Bolan insisted. "Then radio the gunship pilots at Carmiel. We need to transport the prisoners, and I want these fires put out before the whole place burns to the ground."

"You're in charge," the captain replied. He was glad the mysterious fighting machine was on his side as he reached for the two-way radio on his belt.

KATZ HEADED for a house on the western flank, Uzi braced across his prosthesis. One paratrooper accompanied the one-armed commando while the other man under Katz's command supplied cover fire for the pair. They approached a building that had been battered by nearby explosions and assaulted by the fog of thick smoke from the fiery remains of the motor pool. No shots had been fired from the house since the pair had charged from cover.

"You take the back door," Katz ordered. "I'll go in the front. Use a concussion grenade before you go inside just in case they're playing dead in there."

"Right," the trooper said with a nod. "Please remember that I'll be coming from the rear of the house. Try not to mistake me for a terrorist."

"I'll do my best," Katz assured him with a faint smile.

The Phoenix Force warrior moved to the front entrance and waited for the soldier to get into position. Katz tasted smoke when he inhaled deeply to try to keep calm in the stressful situation. He exhaled slowly and felt tension ease from the knot in his stomach. The battlefield was a familiar environment for Katz, and he was no stranger to highly charged emotions stimulated by combat.

The sound of a concussion blast and the fierce vibrations along the wall signaled that the paratrooper had reached the back door and had tossed in the grenade. Katz didn't hesitate. He kicked open the door and charged across the threshold—almost tripping over a corpse on the floor.

Dust and papers swirled within the room as Katz examined the effects of the concussion blast. Furniture had been knocked over, and fragments of adobe dropped from the ceiling. Two figures stirred among the wreckage. One Samson Warrior staggered around in a dazed manner, a Galil rifle clutched in one fist as he clasped the other hand to the side of his bleeding skull. The other terrorist crawled to a canvas bag in a corner of the room.

The man with the rifle presented a clear and present danger because he was already armed. Katz couldn't take any chances under the circumstances and opened fire. A burst of 9 mm slugs smashed into the gunman's chest and sent him hurtling backward through a shattered window. The corpse tumbled over the sill and dropped from view.

Katz turned to face the second terrorist, who was on his feet and holding an odd contraption in his fist. Katz glimpsed a blur of movement as the Samson thug lashed out with the weapon. Leather straps struck the Uzi and steel hooks clawed at Katz's fist. The submachine gun fell from the Stony Man veteran's grasp as he yanked his hand free of the painful sharp metal. Blood dripped from two gouges in his flesh.

Ezra Avriel snarled at Katz, blood flowing from his ears and nostrils. Yet his eyes were bright with fanatical glee greater than the agony of ruptured eardrums and sinuses. He raised the vicious cat-o'-nine-tails and attacked.

Katz shuffled backward and blocked the attack with his artificial arm. The scorpion whip struck metal and plastic, and its hooks tore fabric and scraped against the prosthesis. Straps snared the limb, and Avriel yanked hard to try to pull Katz off balance. The Phoenix leader moved with the pull and suddenly closed in. He stamped a boot against Avriel's kneecap and chopped the side of his hand across the terrorist's forearm.

"Bastard!" the terrorist hissed with anger and pain.

The karate chop failed to knock the whip from Avriel's grasp. Katz broke free of the lash, and Avriel slashed with the scorpion, aiming at the Phoenix fighter's face. The prosthesis rose to meet the whip. Leather and steel hooks tore at the sleeve and the mechanical arm, but failed to strike the older man's face.

Katz stepped in and drove a punch into the right side of his opponent's body. The blow caused sharp pain in the man's liver, and he groaned and staggered, limping on his injured leg. Katz stayed on his opponent and hooked his fist into the side of the Samson extremist's face.

Avriel tried to swing the whip, but Katz was too close to use the lash effectively. The terrorist slammed the wooden handle into the commando's right shoulder, the blow knocking him three steps backward. Avriel slashed the scorpion in a cross-body stroke aimed at Katz's head. The battle-hardened pro ducked, and the lash passed above his skull. Hooks snared the beret from Katz's head and raked his skull.

The prosthesis streaked forward. Katz clamped the trident hooks at the end of the device around the wrist above the whip handle. The steel talons snapped shut, and Katz twisted hard. Avriel cried out as bone cracked in his wrist. Fingers opened, and the scorpion fell to the floor. Avriel swung his free fist at

Katz's face, but the prosthesis delivered a high block to stop the punch.

Katz thrust a palm-heel stroke under Avriel's jaw. The terrorist's head recoiled from the blow and snapped back to expose his throat. The Phoenix leader lunged with the artificial limb once more and grasped Avriel's throat with the hooks. Blood spilled from a punctured artery, and Katz yanked downward to tear out his opponent's windpipe. Ezra Avriel staggered across the room and clutched his ravaged throat with his uninjured hand.

The Samson fanatic dropped to his knees as his life leaked between his fingers. His eyes swelled as he stared down at the scarlet pool that formed on the floor. Katz kicked the scorpion whip and sent it skidding across the room to come to rest in front of Avriel. The terrorist watched his own blood drop onto the torture device.

"Lyova Tuvim says goodbye," Katz announced in a hard voice as Avriel collapsed next to the whip.

A figure appeared at the opposite end of the room. Katz reached for the Walther pistol in shoulder leather, but recognized the paratrooper before he could draw the P-88. His companion stared down at the lifeless body of Ezra Avriel.

"I heard the struggle in here, but I had to dig through some wreckage to get to this part of the house," the soldier explained. "Half the ceiling fell in where I was."

"That's all right," Katz assured him, examining the cuts in the back of his hand. Adrenaline was no longer churning through his veins, and he vividly felt the pain of the wound.

"Are you hurt, sir?" the paratrooper asked.

"Nothing serious," Katz replied, glancing down at Avriel's corpse. "Let's see how they're doing outside."

THE BATTLE WAS OVER. Surviving members of the Samson Warriors were bound with plastic riot cuffs and frisked for weapons. Bolan was pleased to discover none of the Israeli paratroopers had been killed or seriously injured. Katz's torn hand was the worst wound suffered by the assault unit. A medic tended to the ragged cuts and warned Katz that the hand would need some stitches.

"As long as you don't have to amputate, I'll be happy," Katz assured him.

Bolan searched the faces of the captive terrorists. He recognized several men from the Samson Warriors' files supplied by U.S. intelligence and police sources. However, Levi Birnbaum wasn't among them. Bolan asked Captain Moshin if Birnbaum had been identified among the dead terrorists.

"Not yet, but many of the bodies were burned or blown apart or otherwise mutilated beyond recognition. Birnbaum is probably here somewhere."

"We have to be sure," the Executioner stated.

He scanned the kibbutz buildings and frowned. Several houses had been destroyed, and others had been badly damaged. One of the structures was the Samson Warriors' headquarters for the converted base. Bolan hoped it was still standing and that useful information remained inside.

The majority of the terrorists had been housed in the structures on the flanks. Bolan considered this a sign that Birnbaum had operated his camp in a fairly standard manner with the command building at the center and the troops positioned around it. Fortunately the majority of the houses in the middle of the kibbutz had suffered less damage than the other buildings.

He picked the house closest to the dead center of the camp as the most likely choice for the headquarters and, accompanied by Katz, headed out.

Aside from being riddled by machine gun bullets and coated with soot from the fires, the dwelling appeared to be in fairly good condition compared to the other houses.

"Any idea what we're looking for?" Katz inquired, his bandaged hand automatically resting on the frame of his Uzi.

"Not really," Bolan admitted, "but if we find any documents, records, logs or whatever, they might be written in Hebrew. Birnbaum's an American, but he speaks and reads Hebrew fluently. He gave his public speeches in Hebrew as well as English, so he must have kept up with his linguistic skills."

"You're still referring to Birnbaum in the present tense," Katz observed. "So you still think he's alive and not one of the mangled dead."

"Until we have positive ID on the guy," Bolan replied. "If he's dead, we'll just waste a little time searching for the whereabouts of a corpse. If he's still alive, we have to find him."

"Either way we need to search the buildings anyway for evidence for the Israeli authorities to use when they take the terrorists to court," Katz remarked, reaching into a pocket for a penlight.

"Yeah. I'll be glad to hand this mess over to them as soon as I'm sure we've completed our mission here."

Katz understood. He and Bolan were fighting men. They'd spent most of their lives as professional warriors of one sort or another. They'd been forced to give up the comforts of a normal life and devote themselves to fighting campaigns that few would ever know about, yet had to be won.

The mission had to be carried out to the very end because they weren't men to leave a job unfinished. It wasn't enough to cut off the heads of a hydra. The monster had to be totally destroyed or the heads would simply regenerate. The Samson Warriors would regrow new "heads" if Birnbaum escaped and the organization wasn't utterly crushed.

The pair entered the house. The generators that supplied the kibbutz with electricity had been knocked out during the battle, so they used the illumination

provided by their penlights to search the darkness
within. A set of dumbbells, a barbell and a bench press
in the front room suggested that Bolan's guess that the
house had been the base HQ was correct.

Birnbaum was a weight lifter, and the exercise gear
could have been his. Bolan and Katz then discovered
a desk with a cork bulletin board on the wall nearby.
Whatever had been tacked on the board was gone. The
Executioner moved to the desk and tried to open the
drawers. They were locked, but he easily jimmied the
latches with the blade of his Ka-bar.

"Looks like this might have been Birnbaum's office," Katz commented as he inspected a closet.
"Anything interesting in the desk?"

"The drawers are empty," Bolan answered. "Not
even a paper clip."

He checked the ink blotter, but didn't find any
scribbled notes, phone numbers or even doodlings.
The office seemed to be a dead end as Bolan vainly
searched for clues. Then the beam of his flashlight fell
upon a wastebasket by the desk.

The trash container was made of metal, and Bolan
noticed that something had been burned in the can. He
dumped the contents on the floor and sorted through
ashes and charred pieces of paper. He finally found
part of a sheet of newspaper.

"This is printed in Hebrew," Bolan announced.

Katz examined the scrap. "This is from yesterday's
paper. Unfortunately it doesn't have anything except

the date and part of a headline. Are there any other bits of paper?"

"Only ashes, and they've been ground up fairly well. Someone did a pretty fair job of burning this newspaper."

"Not quite good enough," Katz commented. "I doubt Birnbaum intended to roast marshmallows in his office, so he obviously set fire to the paper in an effort to destroy it."

"I was hoping we'd find a bigger clue than this," Bolan admitted, "but we'll just have to make do with what we've got and hope it'll be enough."

15

The Mossad had a major base of operations in Upper Nazareth, which was a small town—compared to Nazareth—that was seldom visited by tourists. The base in the hills was used as a command center for surveillance operations along the Golan Heights.

Mack Bolan and his allies arrived at the base shortly before dawn. Wounded terrorists were delivered to a military hospital, and the healthier prisoners were locked in special security cells. Bolan and Katz took advantage of the opportunity to get some much needed sleep. Captain Moshin would have to deal with his fellow Mossad members at the site and get whatever rest he could later.

After a three-hour nap, Bolan awoke to the sound of a fist pounding on the door to his room. He rolled off the couch and grabbed the .44 Magnum pistol that lay on a chair next to the sofa. His mind was instantly alert, and he realized he was in a small office in a Mossad building. It was unlikely he was in danger of attack.

"Pollock!" a familiar voice called out as the doorknob rattled against the backrest of a chair jammed under it. "This is Moshin. Open up! I have the newspaper!"

Bolan put the gun away and pulled the chair from the door. Moshin entered, a cup of steaming coffee in one hand and a bagel with cream cheese in the other. A folded newspaper was tucked under the man's arm.

"I brought you breakfast," he announced, handing the cup and bagel to Bolan.

"Thanks." The Executioner took the gifts. "What newspaper did you bring?"

"Yesterday's issue of the *Ha'aretz*," Moshin answered. "Why did you jam the doorknob with a chair?"

"Because I didn't have a key to the lock," Bolan replied. "You say this newspaper is from yesterday?"

"Day before yesterday to be precise," Moshin stated. "But I don't think the morning paper has reached the stands in Upper Nazareth."

"Does the headline match the scrap of paper we found at the terrorist camp?" Bolan asked, cutting off Moshin before he could ramble.

"Exactly," the captain confirmed as he unfolded the paper. "We just checked the date and partial headline with the newspapers at the morgue. The *Ha'aretz* matched. It was one of the first papers we checked because it's one of the biggest publications in Israel."

"Good work," Bolan told Moshin as he looked at the front page of the newspaper. He didn't understand the Hebrew letters, but two pictures caught his attention. One beneath the headline depicted police officers surrounding three shroud-covered bodies on the sidewalk. Bolan guessed the photo had been taken in Tel Aviv after the sniper attack on the Samson Warriors advocates.

The other picture was of a man familiar to people throughout the world. He had aquiline features and cold, hard eyes and wore the trademark checkered keffiyeh of a Palestinian. Bolan immediately recognized the face of Munir Kmed.

"You notice the story on Kmed?" Moshin inquired. "It says he's expected to attend a conference of Arab leaders in Beirut to discuss the growing hostilities between Jews and Arabs since the wave of terrorism occurred here."

"An Arab conference?" Bolan asked, intrigued by the news. "Like the one Mubarak held in Cairo after Iraq invaded Kuwait?"

"The reason is similar," Moshin explained. "This conference will be on a much smaller level, and only four Arab nations are sending representatives. None of the heads of government will attend, but Kmed plans to be there because the PLO is being accused of being responsible for the terrorist attacks we know to be the work of the Samson Warriors."

"Kmed would certainly be a tempting target for the Samson Warriors," Bolan said with a nod. "Birnbaum isn't stupid. He knows we're after him."

"Even if he doesn't know exactly who we are," Moshin remarked. "Of course, you're assuming Birnbaum is still alive. Many of the bodies from the terrorist base won't be identified for some time. You saw the condition of those corpses."

"Yeah," Bolan answered, "but there's still a chance Birnbaum wasn't there when we hit the place. That seems even more likely now. If he plans to strike at this Arab conference, he would have to use a fairly small number of men. A large group would attract too much attention at the Lebanese border. He'd also want his people in place in advance of the conference in order to scout out the area before trying any sort of hit."

"That would be quite a different tactic from what the Samson Warriors did in Tel Aviv and the West Bank," Moshin said with a frown. "It's possible they had the newspaper simply because the sniper shooting was one of the headlines of the *Ha'aretz*. A number of eyewitnesses were interviewed by the paper. Most spoke sympathetically about the Samson Warriors. After all, the victims were supporters of Birnbaum's movement and the gunman appeared to be an Arab. The terrorists were probably pleased by the material they read in the paper. An editorial also supported the Samson Warriors as well as three letters from readers."

"Maybe Birnbaum was reading his reviews and maybe he wasn't," the Executioner remarked. "I still suspect Avriel carried out that sniper attack on his own. It was too careless to have had Birnbaum's approval. I doubt he was thrilled with the newspaper coverage because he knew Avriel had jeopardized their organization even if the press didn't. Birnbaum must have realized we'd find his base sooner or later. He might have decided it was time for drastic action against a different target."

"That's a lot of speculation," Moshin insisted. "I know you've been right so far, but I'm not certain we can get much help from the director. Perhaps I should wake Colonel Katzenelenbogen and ask his opinion. He knows Geller better than I do."

"Let Katz get some more sleep," Bolan replied. "Are the prisoners still locked up here?"

"All but the wounded we left at the hospital. They were interrogated most of the night and not permitted to sleep. So far they haven't been very cooperative."

"I want to talk to one of the American terrorists. A private conversation. Okay?"

"That can be arranged."

EUGENE KAMINSKY was escorted into the tiny sound-proof room. A stocky, hard-faced man who still seemed defiant despite being a prisoner, Kaminsky glared at Bolan. The Executioner stood next to a small table and raised a pitcher of water.

"We'll be right outside if you need us," one of the soldiers who escorted Kaminsky announced. "If he gives you any trouble, we'll give him plenty of the same."

"Take the handcuffs off him before you leave," Bolan instructed as he finished pouring the water into two plastic cups.

"That might not be a good idea, sir," the soldier warned. "This man is dangerous, you know."

"He can hold his own cup when he drinks," Bolan insisted. "I don't feel like playing wet nurse with this guy. Just take off the cuffs and wait for me to call you."

The soldiers obliged. Kaminsky rubbed his wrists and flinched when he heard the door slam shut behind him. Bolan placed one cup of water at the edge of the table near a chair.

"Sit down."

"Who the hell are you?" Kaminsky demanded as he folded his arms onto his thick chest. "CIA or some free-lance mercenary bastard they sent to help the Israelis hunt us down? I remember seeing you at the base."

"You're here to answer questions not ask them. Now sit your ass down and have some water. I've got some bad news and you better brace yourself for it."

"I'm touched by your concern," Kaminsky sneered.

The terrorist suddenly charged like a bull. His attack appeared to be an act of mindless frenzy, but he turned as he lunged to throw a left hook at Bolan's face. Kaminsky's big fist missed the mark as the warrior leaned away from the attack. He slammed a heel-of-the-palm stroke against the side of the terrorist's head and sent the startled thug into the table.

Kaminsky's head throbbed from the blow, but he gripped the edge of the table and thrust an awkward karate side kick at Bolan's abdomen. The Executioner easily dodged the clumsy attack and grabbed the guy's ankle, yanking hard and sweeping a boot at Kaminsky's other leg. The terrorist lost his balance and fell to the floor with a painful groan.

The door burst open and two soldiers crowded across the threshold, billy clubs in hand. They were surprised to see Kaminsky on the floor and Bolan calmly standing nearby. The big commando held up a hand to signal the men to stay back.

"I didn't call for you," he told them. "And I thought this room was supposed to be soundproof and I'd have to use the intercom to contact you."

"We felt vibrations along the floor," a trooper explained.

"You guys are alert," Bolan replied. "But wait outside. I can handle this guy."

The soldiers reluctantly departed and closed the door. Kaminsky had gotten to his feet and decided he needed an equalizer to take out Bolan. He grabbed the chair and tried to use it for a club, but the furniture was bolted to the floor and refused to budge.

Bolan stepped forward and hit the terrorist in the side of the jaw with a hard right cross. Kaminsky's head snapped sideways, and he tasted blood. Bolan drove a left hook into his adversary's solar plexus and the man doubled up with a gasp. The Executioner grabbed the guy's arm and twisted it back into a hammerlock. He held the terrorist's wrist up to the shoulder blades with one hand and seized the back of Kaminsky's neck with the other. He then shoved his opponent's head down and pressed his chin over the backrest of the chair. The terrorist tried to struggle, but the pressure of the backrest rim against his throat choked him into surrender. Bolan shoved the guy into the wall and stepped back.

"Bet you can use that water now," Bolan commented. "Sit in the chair and stop acting tough. Come at me again and I'll kill you, and talk to one of your buddies instead."

Kaminsky sat in the chair and gulped down the cup of water. He avoided looking up at Bolan because he knew fear would be telegraphed by his expression. Bolan took a seat at the corner of the table and waited for the guy to catch his breath.

"Okay," he began. "I told you I had some bad news. Your fearless leader Levi Birnbaum ran into a little trouble in Lebanon. He and some of your comrades were captured at the border."

Kaminsky raised his head and stared at Bolan with surprise.

Bolan smiled. "Birnbaum sold you out, pal. That's how we knew where your base was located. Birnbaum squealed like a stuck pig. He told us about the kibbutz and even assured us there were no women and kids there so we could hit you as hard as we wanted without worrying about innocent bystanders.''

"I . . . I don't believe you.''

"You don't, huh?'' Bolan replied with a shrug. "How the hell do you think we found you guys? Figured we used a Ouija board? Grow up, pal. Birnbaum marked the kibbutz out on a map for us. He thinks if he cooperates the Israeli government will cut a deal with him when he goes to court. Birnbaum is hanging you guys out to dry.''

Kaminsky glanced down at the floor. Bolan didn't know if the guy knew he was lying, but the terrorist didn't appear to consider the story impossible. If Birnbaum had been killed during the raid on the kibbutz, Kaminsky wouldn't have any doubt that Bolan was feeding him a line.

"So what the fuck do you want from me?'' Kaminsky asked, still looking at the floor.

"I don't want Birnbaum to get away with cutting a deal,'' Bolan answered. "He masterminded this conspiracy, right? Why the hell should he get off easy while the rest of you guys serve hard time? Probably life in prison. Unless they decide to charge you with treason or espionage against the Israeli government. That's a capital offense here. I think they still execute people by hanging.''

"You want me to rat on my Samson brothers?'' Kaminsky muttered, shaking his head. "No way.''

"Are you really that stupid or just a little deaf?" Bolan asked with a sigh. "The Samson Warriors are finished. We got Birnbaum and you and the other guys at the kibbutz."

"So what can I tell you that you don't already know?" Kaminsky inquired as he drained his cup.

"If you want more water, help yourself," Bolan invited, pushing the pitcher closer to the prisoner. "I'll level with you. Birnbaum hasn't admitted why he was trying to sneak into Lebanon. We figure he was headed for the Arab conference to assassinate the representatives attending the meeting."

"Hell, mister," Kaminsky commented as he poured himself another cup of water, "Levi didn't tell us shit. He and Chaim Stern and some of the other Israelis in our group piled into a couple of our cars and took off. They packed some cameras, tape recorders and stuff like that. We thought that was a little strange, but Levi explained that they had to run a little scouting mission and told the rest of us to sit tight. Claimed he'd be back in a couple of days."

"They didn't take any guns or explosives?"

"Of course they did," Kaminsky answered. "All packed up in duffel bags and stored in the trunk."

The terrorist glared at Bolan. For the first time since the conversation had begun, Kaminsky was suspicious of Bolan's story.

"Wait a minute," the terrorist began. "If you caught Levi in Lebanon, why did you have to ask if he was packing heat?"

"We found Birnbaum and a couple of his play-mates," Bolan lied as fast as his mind could conjure the reply. "We didn't find the cars, and some of the guys with him are still at large. How many went with him for this 'scouting' trip?"

"About a dozen," Kaminsky replied. "Those cars were stuffed, and they used our biggest sedan and a station wagon with the rear seats up."

"I don't suppose you'd know where we could get the license plate numbers for those vehicles?" Bolan asked.

"All I can tell you is the sedan is light blue and the wagon is brown and white," the prisoner answered. "Make that tan and white."

"Okay," Bolan said with a nod. "Birnbaum never mentioned the Arab conference? Never implied that it might be a target?"

"Not really," Kaminsky replied. "Of course, it came up sort of sudden. Not really in our plans, you know. I can tell you this, man, some of the Arab leaders are on Birnbaum's hit list. Assad, King Hussein, Khaddafi, all those guys."

"They won't be at the conference," Bolan said, finally able to say something true to Kaminsky. "What about Kmed?"

"You kiddin'?" The prisoner took a drink of water and continued. "Kmed is right at the head of the list. Birnbaum especially wanted to knock off either Kmed or the leader of the Popular Front for the Liberation of Palestine."

"Why are those two leaders so special?" Bolan inquired, although he had already guessed the answer.

"Because the PLO and the PFLP are outfits set up to force Israel out of existence and reestablish Palestine for the Arabs," Kaminsky explained. "They're political movements with wide sympathy among Arabs throughout the Middle East. If somebody knocked off the leader of an Arab country, people might figure other Arabs did the hit. Just like lots of folks figured Khaddafi probably had Anwar Sadat assassinated for making peace agreements with Israel. But if the heads of the PLO and PFLP get iced, Jews will get blamed for sure."

"Birnbaum *wants* Jews to be accused of murder?" Bolan inquired, eyebrows raised.

"He wants Arabs and Jews to go to war because he says that's the only way Israel will expand and become more powerful. You never heard any of his speeches? The Samson Warriors are based on the concept of Israel becoming a ruling force in the Middle East and an independent world power. That's the only way Jews will ever be really safe and strong. Our Jewish state has to be feared and respected by the rest of the world."

"And killing Kmed would lead to war?"

"The Arab world would condemn the assassination," Kaminsky said. "Even Arab leaders who don't like Kmed or the PLO would have to condemn it because the movement for a Palestinian homeland is an Arab cause. Of course, some other camel jockey would replace Kmed and the PLO would react to his death by carrying out terrorist strikes against Israel. The PFLP would do it, too. Israel would be forced to become more aggressive and claim more territory in order to strike out at terrorist bases."

"Didn't it occur to Birnbaum that Israel could lose a war fought on such a large scale? Instead of creating a bigger and more powerful Jewish state, Israel could be destroyed or the Jews driven out of the country."

"He didn't figure that was possible," Kaminsky said with a shrug. "Birnbaum said the Arab countries wouldn't unite and combine their forces because they're too divided. Even if they did, the United States would back Israel in a war that involved the entire Middle East. He figured Israel couldn't lose. If the Arabs started to win, nuclear weapons would be used. Maybe it would be the end of the world, but that would mean our actions were carrying out prophecies from the Book of Zechariah."

"So you guys figured you'd be carrying out the will of God? You don't seem terribly religious to me, guy."

"Maybe I figured this was a way to make up for what I've done in the past," Kaminsky replied. "My old man always figured I was a disgrace to the family and the Jewish people."

"You should have listened to him," Bolan commented. "Whatever advice your father gave you would have been better than what Birnbaum got you involved with."

"So I fucked up big-time," Kaminsky admitted with a shrug. "I backed the wrong horse, and I'm on the losing end again. You guys will still cut me a deal for cooperating, right?"

"That's not up to me," Bolan answered. "The Israeli authorities will have to decide if what you've told us is worth giving you any slack."

"But you said I could get a deal if I cooperated," Kaminsky declared as he rose from his chair.

"No," Bolan corrected, "I never told you that. This conversation has been tape-recorded. We can play it back to you if you don't believe me."

"But you said Birnbaum..." Kaminsky's expression became pale and he stared at Bolan with eyes wide. "Son of a bitch! You didn't catch Birnbaum! You've been milking me for information so you can hunt him down! Rotten, sneaky bastard—"

"Yeah," the Executioner replied, unconcerned with the terrorist's outrage. "And I want to thank you for being so helpful."

16

Levi Birnbaum carefully peeled the mustache from his upper lip. The spirit gum tugged at his skin until he yanked hard enough to free it. The false mustache and a pair of glasses had served as a subtle disguise along with an oversize straw hat.

Birnbaum and the others didn't remove their disguises until they'd traveled far inland from the Lebanon-Israel border. Forged passports and press identification had allowed Birnbaum and his companions to cross the border without suspicion. Although hastily printed for the trip into Lebanon, the forgeries were good enough to convince the border guards that the men in the sedan and station wagon were a Canadian television news crew.

They'd taken turns driving all night on the roads along the coast. The brisk, salty air from the Mediterranean helped the driver stay awake during the hours of monotonous travel. The team of Samson Warriors finally reached its destination, two miles from Beirut.

Stern had eagerly discarded a camera case and gotten his Beretta 951-R pistol from beneath the front seat of the station wagon. The security chief disliked being unarmed and felt relieved to have the pistol in his belt at the small of his back. Most of the other members of the Samson squad also claimed their side arms as quickly as possible. Birnbaum wasn't fond of firearms and had never acquired much ability with a gun. He didn't carry a weapon as he marched up a hill to observe the area through binoculars.

There were a couple of small villages nearby, but the road was small and seldom used by commercial vehicles, tourists or military convoys. It connected with one of the four major roads that led to Beirut. The soil suffered from erosion, but grass and weeds grew along the hills and sides of the road.

"Perfect," Birnbaum said with satisfaction.

"Not quite," Stern contradicted as he climbed up the hill to join his leader. "The amount of cover is limited if we have to exchange gunfire with the enemy. There are also several small roads similar to this that we have to cover. Our men will be spread thin, and we'll have trouble getting reinforcements to whichever team spots Kmed."

"We'll need more vehicles," Birnbaum commented. "We'll commandeer some cars that are inconspicuous and fast."

"Motorcycles might work better. We'll have a better idea what we'll need after we check the other roads and surrounding terrain. Of course, we'll need to steal at least one car to rig with explosives. I wish we had more time to prepare, Levi. This operation is being rushed too much for my taste. Too many things can go wrong.''

"This opportunity was presented to us like manna from heaven,'' Birnbaum insisted. "It's a message from God, Chaim. We can't fail.''

"I wouldn't be so quick to judge the mind of God,'' Stern warned. "This mission hasn't gone as smoothly as we hoped. Don't count on divine providence to guarantee success.''

"Kmed was delivered to us at the ideal time to salvage our mission,'' Birnbaum stated, unconcerned with Stern's doubts.

He had never had any doubts about their mission. Levi Birnbaum was convinced that his cause was right. He believed the present mission to be his destiny, and nothing could stop him.

KATZ FLEXED his fingers. His hand hurt slightly, but he'd been assured it would heal completely in less than a month. He insisted that the bandages be made thin enough to avoid impairing his dexterity. Katz had to be able to handle a gun if he was to continue the mission in the field.

The one-armed commando reached for a pack of cigarettes as he sat across the desk from Captain Moshin. The Mossad officer had finished speaking with his director on the telephone. Moshin returned the receiver to the cradle and frowned. Katz didn't expect to hear good news.

"All efforts to contact Munir Kmed have failed. The man is like a phantom. He was allegedly in Syria last night, but no one has any idea where he is now."

"Kmed hasn't survived as head of the PLO by being careless," Katz reminded the captain. "He's constantly on the move and never sleeps in the same room two nights in a row. He might have already left Syria."

"That habit makes him a difficult target for his enemies," Moshin admitted, "but in this case it's preventing us from warning him that there could be an attempt to assassinate him if he attends the Arab conference in Beirut."

"If he gets the message from the Mossad, he might not believe it, anyway," Katz remarked as he fired up a cigarette.

"I can hardly believe it myself. I never would have guessed that one day Israeli intelligence would be frantically trying to protect the chief mover and shaker of the PLO."

"It is ironic that Jewish terrorists may kill Kmed because they want to push Israel into war," Katz agreed. "I guess the road to hell is paved by warped intentions."

"If we can't find Kmed, maybe the Samson Warriors won't be able to, either," Moshin said hopefully. "Birnbaum couldn't have known about the conference any sooner than we did and couldn't have predicted Kmed would attend. The assassination plot must have been put together very quickly. They might not even get close to the man."

"Don't count on that," Bolan announced. He'd been studying a detailed wall map of Lebanon and barely glanced at Moshin and Katz. "The prisoner I spoke with said Kmed has been on Birnbaum's hit list for some time. Assassinating him was something they planned to do eventually. This is just an opportunity for them to go after the hit."

"You can't kill a man if you can't find him," Moshin insisted. "In fact, you can't even warn him he's in danger."

"Even if you could contact Kmed, I doubt it will stop him from attending the conference," the Executioner stated. "He knows he's a potential target anywhere he goes. The threat of assassination is nothing new to the man. I don't think he'll back off even if he believes the threat is genuine."

Bolan approached the desk as he added, "I also suspect the Samson Warriors know enough about Kmed to appreciate his paranoid behavior and security that consists of moving from place to place in an irregular manner. They've probably come up with an assassination plan that suits his personality and habits."

"On short notice?" the Mossad officer inquired.

"Not really," Bolan admitted. "Birnbaum probably had some ideas about nailing Kmed that could be modified to fit the right situation. They might not know where he is now, but the Samson Warriors know where he's going. They'll try to hit him when he goes to Beirut.''

"They'll have a hard time getting within half a kilometer of the conference,'' Moshin stated. "Security's very tight. I'm told Jordan and Egypt have sent close to a hundred paratroopers and security agents. Syria has probably sent extra people, as well. That doesn't include the soldiers and security experts Lebanon will supply from their armed forces. They'll probably get additional support from the Arab Deterrent Force and the United Nations Interim Force, which are also stationed in Lebanon.''

"Perhaps Birnbaum doesn't intend to get close to the conference itself,'' Katz suggested. "After all, no government leaders are scheduled to attend. Kmed is the only target they're apt to be interested in.''

"The Samson Warriors have already killed innocent civilians in the West Bank and Tel Aviv,'' Moshin reminded the other men. "Jews as well as Arabs. I don't think they'll hesitate to murder a few representatives from Arab governments in order to get Kmed.''

"Not if there's another way to assassinate him without having to deal with the security forces at the conference,'' Bolan declared. "Kmed probably won't arrive at Beirut International Airport because the terrorism here in Israel has stirred up too many people. Airports are too public, and the press will be swarming the area. Too crowded for good security. Kmed wouldn't arrive there because too many people would know his route from the airport.''

"So he'll go in by car," Katz remarked.

"That's my guess," Bolan confirmed. "I figure he won't want to use the major roads, so he'll use a lesser traveled route of smaller roads until he's actually in Beirut. Birnbaum is probably thinking the same way. He'll station observation teams by the most likely roads and wait for Kmed to show himself."

"I have to admit you've been right so far," Moshin said with a sigh, "but this theory seems like a...a long shot."

"Maybe it is and maybe I'm wrong," Bolan agreed readily. "They've already got hundreds of troops and security experts at the conference site and probably at the airport, as well. All of Beirut will be covered pretty well. There isn't much point in us joining those ranks."

"I pity whoever's in charge of that international collection," Katz commented. "They'll be arguing about who should take orders from whom. Let's not add to the complications. Pollock's idea is worth pursuing."

"The conference is tomorrow morning and we don't know where Kmed is," Moshin reminded the Stony Man pair. "We don't know where the terrorists are, either, and we don't have enough men to properly cover all side roads to Beirut. Don't count on Geller giving us any more. He still isn't convinced Birnbaum wasn't killed at the terrorist base."

"If we can't find the terrorists, we'll have to get them to come to us," Bolan said.

"Any idea how we'll do that?" a puzzled Moshin inquired.

"Yeah. We give them Kmed."

17

The plan required doing research concerning Munir Kmed. Not surprisingly, the Mossad had lots of information about the PLO leader on file. Due to his profession, Mack Bolan already knew a fair amount about Kmed's career. Captain Moshin was a current officer in the Mossad, and Katz had formerly been a field grade in the Israeli intel outfit. Naturally they were more familiar with Kmed's background than Bolan was.

"Is Yakov still studying those videotapes?" Bolan asked the captain.

"I think he's got the gestures and movement mastered. What worries me is the colonel's face. You know, there's no resemblance. If they get a good look at him..."

"I know. The plan's not perfect. A lot of things can go wrong, but we'll try to minimize the possibilities. What about the contacts in Lebanon?"

"The Mossad has lots of people there. It wasn't hard to get the cars you asked for. Just about every VIP from embassy personnel to visiting businessmen are supplied with armor-plated limousines complete with bullet-resistant glass and tires with treated rubber to reduce the likelihood of punctures.''

''Are the volunteers ready?'' Bolan asked.

''Yes. Lieutenant Levitch and his men want to see this through to the end. They all volunteered, and they've been briefed about the assignment.''

''Okay. Let's get everybody together and run through this again. After that we can all get some food and some sleep before we pull out.''

''All right,'' the captain replied. ''I just hope this works. We could be guessing wrong about Birnbaum's next move.''

''We've guessed right so far,'' Bolan replied. ''Let's see how we do this time.''

THE SAMSON WARRIORS WERE in place by dawn. Levi Birnbaum was pleased with his men. They had acquired the necessary extra vehicles and set up observation posts to cover traffic on the side roads outside Beirut. All that was left to do was to wait for Kmed to arrive.

The Samson Warriors leader didn't allow himself to dwell on how the operation could go wrong. He knew Kmed had a private jet and that the PLO head might decide to land at the Beirut airport if he figured security would be better there than on the road. The man claimed to have a ''secret sense'' or ''radar'' that warned him of danger. Whatever else could be said about Munir Kmed, he was definitely a survivor.

Not after today, Birnbaum vowed as he performed some deep-knee-bend squats to work his leg muscles. He still believed Kmed would use a road outside Beirut instead of the airport. Birnbaum's sources had revealed Kmed had been in Syria the day before and was believed to already be somewhere in Lebanon. The Arab had been making more appearances at such political meetings because he was trying to establish the PLO as a respectable organization that represented the Palestinian people. Birnbaum was sure Kmed would attend the conference in Beirut.

Birnbaum's biggest concern was the possibility that they wouldn't recognize Kmed's vehicle when it appeared on the road. The car wouldn't be labeled with a banner waving the colors of the PLO flag. They expected the vehicle to be armored and equipped with bulletproof glass. The latter would probably be tinted glass that would prevent observers from recognizing anyone inside.

It was possible that they'd ambush another VIP on the way to the conference. Birnbaum had no objections to killing a government representative of any Arab country, but only the assassination of Munir Kmed could achieve the results he desired. If they hit the wrong car and killed some obscure diplomat, the Samson Warriors would still have to leave the scene and hope to get Kmed another day.

Levi Birnbaum tried to push such concerns from his mind and cling to his belief that the PLO leader would be delivered to him as part of his destiny to lead Israel into a new status as a mighty world power and the ruling force in the Middle East. With the territories of the Arab nations and the oil fields to provide limitless wealth, Israel would be richer than the U.S. It would become a Jewish empire with undreamed-of power. This was Birnbaum's vision, and he intended to make it a reality or die trying. And Levi Birnbaum wouldn't die alone.

"I've got Unit Three on the radio," Chaim Stern announced, his voice taut with tension. "They claim they've spotted Kmed."

"My God," Birnbaum gasped as he quickly climbed into the front seat next to Stern. "Are they certain?"

"They say they're watching him at this very moment. Talk to them yourself."

Birnbaum eagerly took the transceiver Stern held out and keyed the transmit button. "Unit Three, this is Unit One Command. Over."

"Read you loud and clear, Command," a voice replied. "We have subject under surveillance. Positive ID. We've got the right man. Over."

"Which direction is the car headed?" Birnbaum demanded. "Does it appear to be traveling the road or about to branch off to the main highway? Over."

"Neither at this time. There are two black limousines. Both have parked on the shoulder of the road approximately ten kilometers from our post. Subject emerged from a vehicle and walked up a hill, accompanied by bodyguards. Over."

"You've actually seen him outside the car?" Birnbaum asked, stunned that they would have such a stroke of good luck. "There's no doubt that this is the right man? Over."

"Subject is dressed in military fatigue uniform, boots and a checkered keffiyeh," Unit Three declared. "A side arm is holstered on his hip, and he appears to be wearing gray gloves. Over."

Birnbaum frowned. He didn't recall seeing photos or film footage of Kmed wearing such gloves, but the rest of the description fit their quarry. He keyed the radio.

"Did you see his face clearly?" Birnbaum asked.

"Not really," Unit Three admitted. "The bodyguards are staying close to him while he takes his stroll along the hill. Over."

"Sounds like a precaution in case of sniper attack," Stern told Birnbaum. "They're preventing any hidden gunman from getting a clear target of Kmed's head."

"So you believe this really is Kmed?" Birnbaum asked. "The fact he stopped the car and got out to take a walk around the hill doesn't seem odd?"

"Actually that fits Kmed," Stern explained. "Although the man is forced to be on the move constantly, he tries to maintain some order on a daily level. He tries to exercise every morning and takes walks at a brisk pace for about half an hour before breakfast."

"Then we might really have him," Birnbaum said with a smile. He spoke into the radio. "You said he wears a checkered keffiyeh, Unit Three. How is the head scarf positioned? Over."

"The scarf is draped along one side of his head," the voice replied. "Appears to be deliberately placed that way. Over."

"Munir Kmed wears the keffiyeh hung in the shape of the map of Palestine before it became Israel," Stern remarked, although he knew Birnbaum was aware of this.

"Be careful not to expose yourselves, Unit Three," Birnbaum instructed. "Continue surveillance and keep us posted. Over."

"Affirmative, Command. Over and out."

Birnbaum held the transmit button. "Unit Five? Did you copy on the last transmission? Over."

"Unit Five to Command. Heard it all and am already driving to Unit Three position. Assumed this would be proper response. Over."

"You assumed correctly," Birnbaum confirmed. "Continue to Unit Three and carry out arranged orders. Other units will do their part. Over."

"Understood, Command," the voice of Unit Five answered. "Over and out."

Birnbaum turned to Stern. "How long do you think Kmed will spend at his present position?" he asked.

"He might complete a full half-hour walk or cut it short a few minutes," Stern replied. "Kmed might decide to have breakfast after the walk and make some calls from his car phone or even do a little paper-work. He tries to handle personally as many details of PLO operations and organizational duties as possible. I don't know how safe he'll feel on an open road. Don't expect him to stay long, Levi.''

"The others are already moving in on the bastard. Start the car, Chaim. We don't want to miss the kill."

Stern keyed the ignition and drove forward. He knew the exact location of the other units. The Samson Warriors security chief had a good idea where Kmed had been spotted, and he planned to drive east for fifteen kilometers before pulling onto the same road where Unit Three had reported sighting the limos. This way he could move into position behind the vehicles and cut off any escape route.

"Command, this is Unit Three. The subject has returned to the vehicles with his bodyguards. Over."

"Does he appear ready to continue on to Beirut?" Birnbaum asked. He didn't bother to add "over" at the end of the message.

"Not yet. Subject's companions have set up a folding chair and table near one of the cars. They appear to have given subject a bowl of cereal and poured hot water from a teapot into it. Over."

"Sounds like Kmed's favorite breakfast," Stern told Birnbaum without taking his eyes off the road. "Cornflakes and honey with hot tea poured over it."

Birnbaum grimaced. The man's taste in food didn't sound appetizing to the Samson Warriors leader, but he already considered everything about Kmed to be disgusting. However, the unusual choice for breakfast was even more proof they'd found the right man.

"Everyone's moving into position, Levi," Stern stated. "Better order radio silence from all units. We don't need to communicate now. Everybody knows what to do. Kmed's people might monitor radio broadcasts on different wavelengths and frequencies as part of their security. We don't want them eavesdropping on our conversations."

Birnbaum followed his security man's advice and ordered radio silence. The road was almost deserted, and Stern stepped on the gas pedal. Birnbaum reached into the back seat to gather up a canvas bag that contained an Uzi and some spare magazines. He placed the bag on his lap and pulled down the zipper.

"You probably won't need that," Stern remarked. "If Unit Five gets in place and the limousines travel within range of the car bomb, Kmed and his bodyguards will be taken care of without firing a shot."

"I want to make certain Kmed is dead. I want to be sure that after today war will be inevitable."

18

The limousines rolled along the narrow dirt road at a moderate pace. Mack Bolan sat in the front seat of the lead vehicle. He was dressed in combat gear, complete with holstered pistols, knives, garrotes and grenades. The M-16 with the M-203 grenade launcher attachment was propped near his right hand.

"Next time someone else can play Kmed," Katz groused as he removed the checkered keffiyeh. "Do you know what that concoction of cereal and tea tastes like?"

"Sorry your gourmet taste buds didn't care for the breakfast, but Birnbaum and his people must have done their homework on Kmed. You had to act out his behavior as well as imitate the way he moves and gestures."

Katz had studied the videotapes of Kmed and the information about the PLO leader's habits to play his role in the subterfuge intended to lure the Samson Warriors into attacking the limos. Sunglasses, the keffiyeh and "bodyguards" helped to conceal Katz's features. The biggest flaw in the disguise was Katz's lack of a right hand. Instead of the prosthesis with three steel hooks, Katz wore an artificial "hand" with five metal fingers. It had fewer functions than the hooks, but the "hand" appeared to be made of flesh and blood when covered with a glove, providing one didn't notice that the digits were fixed and rigid.

An observer might wonder why Munir Kmed was wearing a pair of pearl-gray gloves, but the PLO commander was somewhat eccentric. Hopefully the Samson Warriors wouldn't be suspicious about this small detail.

Bolan wondered if the terrorists had even witnessed the little play performed for their benefits. He might have been incorrect when he guessed the enemy would stake out the obscure roads because they expected Kmed to use such a route to Beirut. If so, the security forces in the city might have to deal with Birnbaum and his men.

The Executioner had determined the site for Katz and the paratroopers to pretend to be PLO members by the distance from the roads to Beirut. He tried to estimate where the ambush teams might be located. The Samsons would be posted close enough to the city to be certain traffic was headed into Beirut, but far enough to avoid the army of security personnel assembled for the Arab conference. Bolan planned the "Kmed" performance to be within range of the view of any observation teams posted in the area he suspected the terrorists to be.

Even if the Samson Warriors didn't see the act, there was a good chance they'd attack the limos because the cars would appear to be VIP vehicles headed for the conference. Bolan looked out the windows at the small hills and clusters of grass and weeds. The enemy wouldn't have much cover. It was unlikely they'd launch their primary attack from the hills.

"Stay alert for land mines and other booby traps," Bolan warned Sergeant Segal, who drove the limo. "They might set up roadblocks and use vehicles for cover."

"Yes, sir," Segal agreed with a nod. "Although I wouldn't waste time and ammunition shooting at these limousines if I were in charge of an ambush."

"I don't expect them to, either. Birnbaum and his people will be ready to attack armored vehicles like these. They'll almost certainly use explosives of some sort."

Katz sat in the back seat with two other paratroopers. He was once again armed with his Uzi and Walther P-88. The soldiers had discarded the civilian jackets worn as their former disguise and exchanged the keffiyehs for berets. They were also equipped with weapons and were tensely ready for battle.

Captain Moshin, Lieutenant Levitch and the remaining paratroopers were in the second limo. They were prepared for trouble and watched the rear in case the terrorists attacked from behind. However, they were all beginning to doubt Bolan's theory and suspected that the Samson Warriors weren't in the area.

"There's a car up ahead," Segal announced when he saw the Volkswagen parked on the shoulder of the road.

"I see it," Bolan confirmed. "Make a U-turn and head the other way."

"There doesn't appear to be anyone in the car or behind it," the NCO told Bolan. "It could just be an abandoned vehicle."

"And it could be a car bomb," Katz declared. "Turn around, Sergeant."

The lead limo swung into a U-turn as Bolan ordered him to speed up. The big black car bolted, and the second limo followed its example. The vehicles increased speed, dust spewing from under the whirling tires as the Volkswagen exploded with a powerful roar.

Dirt and stones showered down on the vehicles from the debris hurled by the blast. Automatic gunfire erupted from the top of a hill. Bullets raked the armored sides of the big cars without effect. Bolan glanced out a window and saw the heads and shoulders of figures appear along the summits of hills. The muzzle-flash of an assault rifle revealed the source of the gunfire.

"Keep going!" Bolan ordered. "This isn't a good defense position. If they lob grenades, they can blow us off the road."

"Where *is* a good defense position here?" Segal asked, his voice tense and his fists clutched tightly around the steering wheel.

"THE BASTARDS must have spotted the car bomb," Birnbaum hissed when he saw the limos headed straight for the sedan.

He and Stern had intended to hit their opponents from the rear only to discover the limousines had changed direction, apparently unharmed by the bomb. Stern turned the wheel sharply and spun the car, parking it lengthwise across the road. He realized the sedan wouldn't form a solid barrier for the big armor-plated vehicles, but it might slow the limos down if they had to ram through.

"All units to the Unit Three road!" Birnbaum said into the radio as he emerged from the sedan, transceiver in one hand and Uzi in the other. "The target is getting away! Close in from all sides and both ends of the road immediately!"

"They're already doing that," Stern growled with frustration. The sound of gunfire was evidence that the other Samson Warriors were already aware that the plan had gone sour.

The security chief bolted from the car, hurried to the trunk and opened it to remove an MK-19 grenade launcher. He didn't bother with the Galil rifle in the back seat. Bullets would be as useless as a peashooter against the armored cars.

He saw the first limo slow slightly as it approached. A tall man, dressed in black fatigues suddenly opened the front passenger door and jumped from the car. The man landed surefooted, knees bent to absorb the impact. Stern saw the M-16 and ducked behind the sedan.

Birnbaum began to run for cover behind a cypress tree at the side of the road, spraying a volley of 9 mm rounds at the limos as he ran. Bullets struck the windshield of the closest vehicle, but failed even to crack the thick tinted glass.

Stern swung his MK-19 across the trunk of the sedan and prepared to open fire. He barely glimpsed the muzzle-flash of the man in black's weapon, but realized it didn't come from the rifle barrel. The Israeli saw the M-203 grenade launcher attached to the underside of the M-16 barrel and heard the whistle of a large round. The 40 mm shell smashed into the roof of the sedan and exploded.

Stern's head was blasted from his neck, and his body was mangled with the wreckage of the sedan as the car burst like a water balloon against concrete. The fuel tank exploded, and the force of the blast hit Birnbaum with a powerful shock wave. The Samson leader was thrown ten feet and slammed to earth in a battered, stunned heap.

Flaming gasoline stretched across the road as the first limousine bolted forward. It streaked through the wall of fire unharmed, but discovered two men on motorcycles racing toward the battle scene from the opposite direction.

One cyclist drew a MAC-10 machine pistol from his saddle bag and fired one-handed at the limo. The other motorcyclist removed a grenade from inside his leather jacket and tried to pull the pin with his teeth while trying to operate the handle bars with one hand.

Katz shoved open the limo door and triggered his Uzi, concentrating on the guy with the grenade. The one-armed commando was aware that the explosive was a more serious threat to the limo than the MAC-10. He drilled the target through the chest, the 9 mm manglers punching the terrorist backward out of the saddle.

The Samson Warrior crashed lifeless to the ground as his fellow cyclist tried to steer into position to get a clear shot at Katz. The Phoenix Force leader retreated inside the limo and shut the door. Bullets hammered steel and glass. A spiderweb pattern appeared in the window inches from Katz's face, but the thick glass pane held fast.

Segal turned the steering wheel hard, smashing the nose of the car into the second motorcycle. The terrorist rider shrieked in agony as his right leg was crushed. The impact sent man and machine into a graceless cartwheel across the dirt road.

"Let me out!" Katz ordered, Uzi braced along his prosthesis.

The sergeant stopped the limo, and Katz and the paratroopers jumped from the car. The second limousine screeched to a halt, and Captain Moshin and Lieutenant Levitch emerged, weapons in hand.

"How do we handle this, Colonel?" Moshin asked. "Pollock is on foot and headed up a hill. Do we do the same?"

"Absolutely. The terrorists' only advantage is if they can keep the high ground and take us out by firing down at us and using grenades to blow up the limos."

"The terrorists we saw on the hills will be pursuing on foot," Levitch remarked. "We'd better get up there to stop them."

"Captain," Katz addressed Moshin, "you go with one of the limos and take both cars down the road about a quarter of a kilometer. Set up a barricade to keep other vehicles out of the area. Be ready to take on any extra attackers, and radio Beirut. See if we can get some reinforcements out here. With hundreds of troops and security experts in town, they ought to be able to spare a few."

"Especially since we're doing their job here," Moshin commented.

A TRIO OF SAMSON WARRIORS jogged along the rolling hills in pursuit of the limousines. Only one man carried a grenade launcher, but the others had Galil rifles and packed an assortment of grenades, which hung on their belts and harness gear straps.

In their haste they failed to notice a black shape in the tall grass and unruly weeds. When the men were less than twenty yards distant, the Executioner rose from concealment, Beretta 93-R in one fist and Desert Eagle in the other. He opened fire, pumping a 3-round burst of Parabellums between the shoulder blades of his closest enemy.

The guy pitched forward and collided with a comrade, both men falling to the ground as the third attempted to swing his Galil at Bolan. The Desert Eagle bellowed, and a big .44 Magnum slug split the rifleman's breastbone, churning heart and lungs into bloodied pulp.

The survivor shoved aside the corpse of his fellow terrorist. He barely noticed that the other guy was also dead as he fumbled with the trigger of his MK-19. Bolan fired the 93-R, and the Samson gunner's face disintegrated into a collage of crimson, gray and jagged pieces of bone. Bolan turned as he heard the growl of engines below.

He looked down from the summit and saw an approaching tan-and-white station wagon, accompanied by a motorcyclist. The Uzi in the grasp of the biker and a rifle barrel at the open window of the wagon labeled the vehicles as transport for more members of Birnbaum's hit team.

Bolan holstered the Eagle and removed a grenade from his combat harness. The Executioner pulled the pin and lobbed the M-26 blaster at the station wagon. The deadly orb landed in the path of the wagon, and the vehicle rolled over it. The grenade detonated, tearing into the belly of the car. The concussive force hurled the vehicle into the air.

It fell to the ground in a nosedive, performing a brief balancing act, standing upright for a split second on its grille. Metal crumpled and the car crashed down onto its roof. Window glass shattered, and the windshield popped loose from the dented frame-work. Tires spun uselessly in the air as the wagon lay upside down like a giant beetle unable to right itself.

The explosion had stunned the biker. He lost control of his motorcycle and crashed into the side of the hill. Bolan pointed his Beretta at the man, who lay spread-eagle, either dead or unconscious. The man was down and out.

Gunfire from the hills on the opposite side of the road revealed that more Samson Warriors had reached the scene. Bolan recognized Katz and Moshin among the combatants. Only two terrorists confronted the one-armed Phoenix veteran and his allies. The pair were pitted against too much firepower and skill to last for long.

Bolan turned to retrieve his M-16, hidden in the foliage where he'd confronted the terrorist trio. A massive form suddenly rushed toward him. Bolan brought the Beretta into target acquisition, but before he could get off a shot, a rock-hard fist slammed into his forearm. The blow jarred the ulnar nerve and sent the 93-R hurtling from numb fingers.

Levi Birnbaum's face was bruised and bloodied, but his eyes burned with rage. He'd failed to find his Uzi when he recovered consciousness, but climbed up the hill to confront Bolan, armed only with his exceptional physical strength.

A big fist rocketed for Bolan's face, but the Executioner dodged the punch and lashed out with his booted foot. His heel struck Birnbaum above his kidney. The terrorist groaned and lunged, hands clawing at his adversary.

Bolan recoiled, then slashed a side-of-the-hand stroke at the larger man's face.

Birnbaum feinted toward Bolan's ribs, then swung a left hook at his skull. The Executioner's head weaved away from the punch. Air rushed into his face as the fist slashed less than an inch from his nose.

Bolan hit his opponent with an overhead right, his knuckles striking Birnbaum in the cheekbone. The blow stunned the big terrorist, but it didn't hurt him. Bolan followed through with a kick to Birnbaum's heart.

The Samson leader hissed with pain and swept an arm at the Executioner, which hit Bolan in the chest like a hammer. The blow lifted him off his feet and dumped him onto his back.

Stunned and winded by the powerful strike, the Executioner looked up at Birnbaum. The terrorist smiled and stepped closer. He raised a size fourteen boot and prepared to stomp the life from his dazed opponent. Bolan braced himself at the small of his back and kicked out with both legs. One boot slammed into Birnbaum's calf to deflect the terrorist's attack. The warrior's other foot caught the Samson fanatic squarely in the crotch.

Birnbaum wheezed in agony and stumbled backward, nearly losing his balance. The bare-handed battle had gone far enough for Bolan's liking, and he reached for the .44 Magnum.

The terrorist saw the move and suddenly charged, losing all the self-control he thought he'd acquired over the years. He reached out for Bolan's throat, his only desire to throttle his opponent.

Bolan sidestepped the frenzied attack and drew his pistol. As Birnbaum staggered past his intended victim, the warrior slapped the steel barrel of the Desert Eagle across the man's skull. The forceful blow knocked the terrorist to his knees.

"It's over, Birnbaum," the Executioner announced as he pointed the .44 at his adversary. "You lost."

The terrorist stared at Bolan with watery eyes. Blood oozed from his nostrils and a cut above his eyebrow. He blinked and slowly started to rise. The Executioner kept his weapon trained on the muscular madman. He stayed eight feet away to remain out of reach of any desperate attempt to grab or to kick at his gun hand.

"Who are you?" Birnbaum asked in a croaking voice. "How the hell did you know where we'd be?"

"Does it matter?"

"I guess not. You're an American. Who are you working for?"

"Just get your hands up," Bolan growled.

The Samson leader slowly raised his hands to shoulder level. Then he suddenly pitched himself sideways and fell to the ground near the corpses of the three Samson Warriors Bolan had taken out earlier. The Executioner hadn't opened fire because Birnbaum's motion had been away from him. However, he saw the reason for the terrorist's actions.

Birnbaum had landed beside the Galil rifle of one of his dead comrades. He grabbed the weapon and started to swing the barrel toward Bolan. The Executioner had already aimed his pistol. The Desert Eagle roared, and a .44 Magnum slug blew a hole through Birnbaum's skull. The Galil clattered next to the ground as Birnbaum's body performed a violent spasm. The body-builder muscles convulsed for three full seconds before accepting the fact that the man was dead.

Bolan joined the rest of the team by the limousines. One of the Israeli paratroopers had been killed in the shoot-out with the terrorists, but he was the only casualty.

Katz canted his Uzi across a shoulder and nodded a greeting. Bolan returned the gesture. They'd survived another battlefield, and yet another enemy had been defeated. Moshin and the troopers had two Samson Warriors held prisoner at gunpoint. The rest of the terrorist outfit was dead.

"We didn't find Birnbaum," Moshin told Bolan.

"I did," the Executioner assured him. "Let's get the hell out of here."

**The Peacekeepers do not
negotiate peace—
they impose it.**

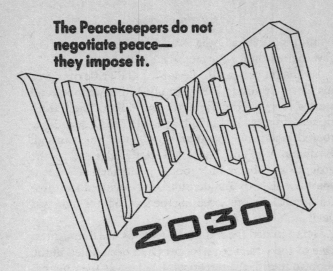

WARKEEP

2030

MICHAEL KASNER

**The year is 2030 and the world is in a state of extreme
political and territorial unrest. Under a joint Russian-
American initiative, an elite military force—The Keepers—
has been dispatched to contain the damage. With the
ultimate in 21st-century weaponry, they complete their
mission: strike first, strike hard and give no quarter.**

WK1

Dan Samson finds himself a deciding factor
in the Civil War in the third thrilling
episode of the action miniseries...

TIMERAIDER

John Barnes

Dan Samson, a hero for all time, is thrown into
the past to fight on the battlefields of history.

In Book 3: UNION FIRES, the scene has switched
to the Civil War, and Vietnam veteran Dan
Samson works to free a leading member of the
biggest resistance group in the South.

Available in December at your favorite retail outlet.

In the 21st century, a new breed of cop
brings home the law in the latest
installment of the future law-enforcement
miniseries...

MIKE LINAKER

In the 21st-century nightmare, marshals like Thomas
Jefferson Cade carry a badge, a gun and a burning
sense of justice.

In Book 3: FIRESTREAK, Cade and his cyborg partner,
Janek, follow the bloody trail of a renegade drug
dealer to the electronic wonderland of Los Angeles and
enter the killzone... guns loaded, targets in sight.

Available in January at your favorite retail outlet.